SYBIL NORCROFT BOOK TEN

THE STRUGGLE

A FIGHTING WOMAN AGAINST ALL ODDS

I0549027

CARL DOUGLASS

NEUROSURGEON TURNED AUTHOR WRITES WITH
GRIPPING REALISM

PUBLICATION
CONSULTANTS
We Believe In The Power Of Authors

PO Box 221974 Anchorage, Alaska 99522-1974
books@publicationconsultants.com, www.publicationconsultants.com

ISBN Number: 978-1-63747-037-4
eBook ISBN Number: 978-1-63747-038-1

Library of Congress Number: 2021951319

Front cover photo ©Jeff Schultz/SchultzPhoto.com

Manufactured in the United States of America

CHAPTER ONE

The PDB was short and to the point. The DNI told the president about a meeting at the Kremlin during which she was described as a "pushover" because she had allowed the British to humiliate her with their naval and bombing attacks. Tikhondnko had echoed the charge by revealing intel from within a supposedly secret bipartisan meeting held in The Canyons Sky Resort in Park City, Utah. There was one item on the agenda of that meeting—how to proceed with impeachment. The Russian President Afonsaii Glebovich Tikhondnko asked the pivotal question: Is now not the time to expand in the Ukraine?"

CIA agents have identified known members of the IPA [*Sluzhba vneshney razvedki Rossiyskoy Federatsii*], Russia's external *intelligence* agency, on the streets of cities in the Crimean peninsula, the Donbas region of eastern Ukraine, and in Kiev itself.

"Alt-right followers and members of the base of former prime minister Benjamin Wood-Jackson were quietly holding clandestine meetings to resurrect Wood-Jackson's reputation. A former deputy defense minister was quoted as saying, 'He's our Napoleon stuck on Elbe waiting for his February, 1815. We must give him his Napoleon brig *Inconstant* and his 700 good men.'

"Our agents are seeing posters tacked on telephone poles, the sides of empty buildings, and glued to post office boxes. They read, 'Give Ben Wood-Jackson his brig *Inconstant* and his February, 1815!' The gendarmes cannot tear them down as fast as the base can put them up. It is our opinion that there is a new groundswell to bring him out of seclusion to save Great Britain, despite the fact that he has not been seen nor heard from since being ousted from office.

"The PRC hackers are mounting a covert campaign to force the resignation of Martin Angleton, the secretary of the treasury and to spread a rumor—gaining some legs, I might add—that dozens of good vice-presidential candidates have turned President Daniels down because she is 'a weak-kneed, ineffective, effete, rich, girl who has no business trying to run a country.'"

The PDB ended precisely at 0700; and for some reason, the president did not feel like having a nice White House breakfast.

The first scheduled meeting of the day was with the leaders of the most important unions in the country: AFL-CIO, Hoyt Allred; Teamsters, Butch Ed Jenkins; CtW, Miriam R. Cohen; and IWW, Achmed ibn Hafeez; and her secretary of labor, Randy Eilson. They met in the Oval Office.

CtW [Chance to Win, offshoot of the AFL-CIO] Cohen had been elected spokesperson by the union bosses, and she began to speak even before Sybil could greet the group.

"Madam President, this is a courtesy call to let you know that we are in the process of declaring a nationwide union strike and to make it grow into a general strike of all oppressed American workers. Businesses are closing faster than we can keep count, and us workers are bearing the brunt of that aspect of the depression that we had nothing to do with. The reconstruction work is going on faster and faster all the time, but we union people are being left behind. That is not fair. We have worked long and hard to get our people decent livings and skills that make them crucial to the country.

There's no way we can compete with volunteer labor, and there's no way the construction projects done by volunteers will meet union or legal standards. It has to stop; the reconstruction of America has to be a union shop project if we have any chance of getting it done right and in a timely fashion. We demand standard union pay and benefits, and we demand that it start yesterday. Literally, we want compensation for the time union labor was denied its right to participate and be paid."

Secy. Eilson gave a rebuttal, "Hello Miriam, good to see you again. It has been a while. Our people in Commerce have been following the rebuilding process and trying to understand and to deal with all its complexities. First of all, this is not strictly a government project; it is an American national project. Second of all, it was imperative that we hit the road running; and we did not have time for lengthy contractual negotiations with unions and employers. Third, the project of rebuilding our country has been one of President Daniels's key programs. As a result of all that has happened, she declared a national emergency which is still in effect. Lastly, she has fought tooth and toenail with Congress to ensure that the treasury could open its vaults to get the needed money. As a matter of fact, Congress right now is starting a discussion about impeachment because they think she did not involve them enough. She did it the way she did because she knew that Congress is not in the business of getting things done. They debate.

"We did not have time for the niceties of contract talks or debates. We had the terrible task of getting America back on its feet and its economy going again. Once the riots and destruction were over, the paramount need for this administration has been to build, not dither, even if a few toes get stepped on. And, I'm sure you know, the treasury supply has pretty much run dry."

"It's our toes that are getting stepped on, Mr. Secretary. Try and put yourselves in our shoes," said Teamsters boss," Butch Jenkins in his gravelly voice.

"Pretty much everybody is wearing the same kind of shoes. What would not be fair is for the unions to benefit at the expense of the rest of the workers of the country, many of whom are volunteering their time to get us back on our feet; so, there will be jobs at all, let alone high paying union jobs."

"There you go again," Hoyt Allred from the AFL-CIO piped in. "It's always the unions' fault, or the rich and corrupt unions are trying to fleece the nice employers' organizations, or the greedy union workers want more money for less work and more chance to feather bed than the rest of the nation's workers. Well, it won't work this time. We have unions and union laws to protect us. We will have our due; or this administration of political hacks, the greed-driven employers, and the lazy, nogood-fornothing bums on the dole will learn the reason why."

His face was red, and his demeanor threatening, which was his usual negotiating tactic. The Oval Office did not allow such aggressiveness. One of President Daniels's Secret Service guards moved quietly between Allred and the president and gave the union leader the evil eye. He got the hint and backed off.

"So, Madam President," asked IWW's Achmed ibn Hafeez, "what's your response to all of this? You're the one in the cat bird's seat. How are you going to do to make this right?"

Sybil had been quiet and patient up to that point, and it was her turn to speak, in fact, to get in the last word.

"Union leaders, I address my comments to all of you and all of the union leaders and union members across America. I sympathize with your cause. In a more nearly perfect world and at a much better time, the country and me as the lady in the cat bird seat—as you term it—would side with your argument. The times are far from perfect, and the needs of the nation are immense. Nothing approaching normal will return to this country unless and until we get the country back on its feet. Everyone is going to have to give something, give up something, make sacrifices, and pitch in. I have a question for all of you before I tell you where the bear sleeps. What are you unionists going to do?"

"We're gonna fight," President Cohen said with a near snarl on her lips.

"Fight whom?" Sybil asked calmly.

"Big business, the money mongers, and the government lackies!"

"Are you going to pitch in and help the rest of the loyal Americans who are already hard at work." Sybil asked reasonably, ignoring the slur of her being a lacky.

"We're goin' on strike, the biggest strike in the history of the world, Madam," said Allred, and despite himself, he moved towards the lady president.

Two Secret Service guards moved between the union leader and the president and began to move Allred away from her to a point ten feet from the entrance door to the Oval Office and twenty feet away from the woman they had an oath to protect, even to take a bullet for. He was chastened and apologized.

"I take it that you are not going to help your fellow Americans; you are not going to accept reasonable reduction in pay during this ongoing crisis; and that you are still going to go ahead with a crippling strike despite all Secretary Eilson and I have told you."

"You got it, Lady," said the thick-necked Butch Jenkins.

"Then, in my capacity as the president and commander-in-chief of the armed forces during a clear and present danger of anarchy and economic collapse, I am here to inform you and everyone you represent that every man or woman who strikes will be considered a criminal, arrested, and placed in detention under the Security In Time of Crisis Act. That is my last word on the subject. You have been warned.

She turned to her two guards, "Please show the lady and these gentlemen out of the office and out of the People's House.

"Good day to each of you."

Secretary Eilson waited until he and the president were alone.

"Madam President, if I may, I have a suggestion."

"Please."

"In my opinion, we have not heard the last of this. In fact, I predict a test by the unions of your resolve now that you have laid down the gauntlet. Knowing those people as I do, I expect that we will see a union shut down in New York City accompanied by some selective violence—enough to see if you will send in the cavalry to quell the disturbance and to get the city's economy back on track."

"Seriously, after I put the nation on martial law and enforced it with national guard, police, national guard, and regular active duty armed forces personnel? Wasn't that demonstration enough, Randy?"

"With respect, Ma'am, no. This is different, more nuanced and focused. The union members are not setting out to foment a riot, just a demonstration of sorts; their kind of sorts which begins with a strike, followed by strike breakers. They will argue that they are law-abiding unionists striking as is their right."

"So, do you have a suggestion?"

"Don't be fooled. This will be a hard-core microcosm of what happened on a national scale. Will you step in with hobnail boots against the poor oppressed union bosses and their minions or let them control the narrative."

"I guess I'll have to opt for the hobnail boot approach, much as I dislike the characterization."

"You know, Madam President, this could be an entering wedge answer to your issues with the Congress. While they debate and dither, you once again have to defend the Constitution and New York City; and you have to do it now, i.e. the day the inevitable strike starts. They want to know if you fear losing the union and their supporters' votes or New York more."

"I'll have to get one of my administration's political hacks to go out to REI and buy me a pair of chic hobnail boots to go with my designer black dress and make ready for the confrontation."

"If I get the chance, Madam President, I will surely vote for your re-election…as many times as necessary."

He pushed his tongue into his cheek to make his point.

CHAPTER TWO

President Daniels's little grandson, Bonheur, had a difficult time with his aseptic meningitis. His first day in the pediatric ICU, he had a grand mal seizure associated with a fever of 104 degrees which left him stuporous for a day. Sybil sneaked away from the White House to visit the little boy. Just as she arrived, a nurse abandoned her effort to get an IV in, handed the task to the pediatrician who similarly failed leaving the little boy's arms and his scalp dotted with pin holes. The good thing about it was that the repeated pains got him awake and screaming. They were waiting for the pediatric anesthesiologist to arrive when she finished the operation she was working in.

"Gamma," Bonheur cried when he saw her. I wants to go home, and you take care of me."

"Sorry, Bub, you have to stay here. And you need to have an IV."

"My doesn't want a iravee, Gamma. Let's go home."

He began to cry softly and could not stop.

Sybil looked at the pediatrician and said, "How about I give it one try. I have an idea."

He looked at her with consternation.

She said, in her best Jewish kvetching voice, "Can't hoit, might help. Better even than chicken soup."

The pediatrician nodded his head; who was he to refuse the president of the United States?

He ordered the door locked and the blinds closed.

Sybil pressed on the lower left side of Bonheur's neck which caused the large external jugular vein to bulge. She swabbed his neck with antiseptic.

"I am going to give you a little pinchy hurt, Bonheur. It won't be too bad, but you have to hold still, okay?"

"I'll be a good boy, Gamma."

She used a small syringe filled with lidocaine and a 27 gauge needle to deaden a small portion of skin over the enlarged vein. The pain was not nearly as severe as a bee sting, and Bonheur settled down. Next, Sybil took a sharp pointed number 11 scalpel blade and made a small shallow nick in the area of the deadened skin.

"Hand me a 22 gauge catheter, please," she asked the nurse.

She slowly pushed the sharp needle through the skin without hurting the little boy. She maintained pressure on the vein. The needle met a slight amount of resistance, and Sybil pushed quickly, and the needle and cannula filled with blood rewarding the little audience and allowing them to exhale. Sybil carefully pushed the catheter off the needle and up into the vein. She attached the IV to the catheter and sutured the catheter in place.

"Nicely done," the nurse complimented her.

"Okay for my first time, don't you think?" Sybil said, and everyone gave a little relieved laugh.

The catheter was still flowing well when it was time for Bonheur to go home, a much healthier little boy than when he entered the ICU. By some magic of the press, the procedure made the news, complete with iPhone photographs. Sybil's favorability rating jumped five points, and that lasted three days.

The NSA reported that the Middle-East pipeline flow was gradually diminishing in flow, enough to cause Sybil to have another polite talk with Russian president Tikhondnko and Saudi King Al Saud. This time she stated simply that if the flow did not increase to thirty percent above normal level in two days, she would have the United Nations handle the problem and have peacekeepers arrive to guarantee compliance.

"Ve are shore tis ist a minor engineering klitch, Madam President. Ve surely vill not need to haf the United Nations get involved," Tikhondnko said, speaking for both Russia and Saudi Arabia. "Pleze to look at the NSA data over the next duu tays. You vill see improvement, Ve tink."

That promise came to pass.

The ODNI called the Oval Office shortly after Sybil finished her nice talk with the nice Saudis and Russians.

"Good to hear from you Admiral Jacobsen," Sybil said.

"You might not think so when I'm done, Madam President," Adm. Jacobsen said

"Color me surprised," Sybil said with mild sarcasm.

"We need to come to the Oval Office."

Mrs. Carpentier admitted Adm. Jacobsen the DNI, Lt. Gen. Paul R. Reynolds the DIRNSA [Director of the National Security Agency], and the DCIA Martin Obershauer.

The DNI wasted no time on small talk.

"Here goes. KCTV [Korean Central Television, MR: *Chosŏn Chungang T'ellebijyon*] featured its favorite star with an announcement last night, 'The southern lackies have joined with the hegemonists to threaten our dear nation,' Kim Jong Un said. His face was contorted with anger. 'Our small but proud nation shall stand up to the hegemonist bully. This very day, look to your television screens and pay attention to the direction our line of long-distance artillery is pointing.'

This morning, KCTV showed several thousand heavy artillery weapons and fourteen large missiles all inclined towards Seoul, 185 km to the south. Another large assembly of heavy artillery is centered around Namp'o 50 km farther south. There was a typical goose-stepping military parade in Pyongyang. The sabers are raised and rattling. Our people there rate the action as a 5+ on the 1-10 scale of concern."

With less than half a minute's decision time, President Daniels had Mrs. Carpentier summon the CJCS to the office.

The courtesies were observed, then Sybil gave General Glen Gabler, Sr. the CJCS his orders, "General, we need a robust response to the present North Korean saber rattling. I want you to make that communication very clear."

"Madam President, my suggestion is that we do two significant things beginning as soon as I can make the calls: I will dispatch our three carrier strike force groups--the USS *Nimitz*, the USS *Reagan*, and the USS *Theodore Roosevelt*, and have them sit off the coast of the DPRK in international waters. They are actually not far off right now. The entire force can be in place in four hours if they travel full steam ahead. Their instructions will be to prepare for a carrier-based aircraft preemptive strike against North Korea, and their fleet escort ships can stand ready to fire cruise missiles. I will communicate to LTG Bills who is in command of the Eighth Army at Garrison-Humphreys in Pyeongtaek, South Korea and to Gen. Robert Abrams, commander of the United Nations Command, Combined Forces Command and United States Forces Korea based at Osan Air Base, to go to DEFCON 2. This will only be the third time that that level has been ordered. Are we that concerned and committed, Ma'am?"

"Yes, Sir. Do it," said the commander-in-chief.

"Aye-Aye."

Sybil took a few deep breaths once the military officers left her office; so, she could deal with the third snarling enemy of her day—the Congress. She had Mrs. Carpentier arrange a White House meeting with Speaker Zimbrowski and Majority Leader Nichols within the hour.

The two Congressional leaders were disgruntled at what they considered to be a preemptory and discourteous summons, but they both came to the Oval Office in fifty-six minutes.

Neither leader felt any necessity to be overly courteous to the upstart, and unelected president. After all, they reasoned, she was very likely not to be around much longer.

"What is it?" Speaker Zimbrowski demanded to know almost before the office door closed behind her.

"And a good morning to you, Madam Speaker and Leader Nichols. I wanted to inform you of this morning's developments with regards the DPRK [The Democratic People's Republic of Korea]."

The two leaders dropped their sullen facial expressions and listened intently as the president reported the actions she had taken to counteract the bellicosity of the unstable DPRK nuclear situation and the threats.

"Madam President, do you actually intend to launch a preemptive strike and to propel us into what will almost certainly grow to be World War III?"

"I don't, and I did not say that. What I did say was that once we are in place, Kim Jong Un and his military will be aware that any aggressive action on their parts will result in a catastrophe for their poor country. Our military has been ordered not to fire unless fired upon, or unless they receive a presidential order."

"So, the safety of the world rests on your proud shoulders, Madam President. Is that about it?"

"You could look at it that way, or you could think positively that they will back down as they have always done."

"And almost always with a bribe. Is history going to repeat itself on your watch, President Daniels?"

"No bribe. No conditions. The Occam's Razor of this situation is…back down without firing a shot, or be turned to dust."

"Madam President," said a very disturbed Secretary Zimbrowski, "I promised not to divulge this, but you have brought the country to the very brink. We are fashioning a procedure to impeach you, and this recklessness of yours will pour gasoline on the little waste basket fire we have up to now."

"Thank you for stopping by, Madam Secretary and Honorable Majority Leader."

Sybil's final item of business was to inform Kim Yong-nam, the head of state for foreign affairs for the DPRK, of the United States' response to their provocation. It was not a cordial call.

CHAPTER THREE

While the ships were on their way to the Yellow Sea and Korea Bay, and the air force bombers making their way to South Korea's Kunsan Air Base—a United States Air Force base located on the west coast of the South Korean peninsula bordered by the Yellow Sea—and Osan Air Base 240 km south of Seoul, Sybil had to turn her attention to a significant problem that had been escaping her notice.

The Senate had a backlog of 221 overdue appointments throughout the government that were going unfilled, and the government serving the many smaller everyday issues for ordinary Americans was becoming progressively less effective. Sybil's favorability rating was sliding accordingly. It dawned on her that this could not be altogether coincidental or due to senatorial sloth. She wondered what the Senate had been up to.

Two weeks previously, Senate Majority leader Ralph Henry Nichols began holding meetings with both political party leaders on an issue separate from their clandestine inquiry into the potential for impeachment. This inquiry was nefarious so far as the government function was concerned and was intended to impede almost any effort the president tried to keep the government going.

"It is fairly simple, but everyone in this room is going to have to get their fellow senators on board for us to succeed. We have hit something of a barricade on the impeachment progress because we have not been able to agree on good enough wording for anything that sounds even remotely like 'high crimes and misdemeanors'. We'll get there but not as fast as we would like. So, the next option is to make her unfavorable rating increase steadily and seriously. You all know that presidents' get credit for favorable historical occurrences and blame for unfavorable ones like the rise and fall of the economy, whether they are actually responsible. We are going to see that the public becomes angrier and angrier about the function of the government. Joe Public really knows very little about what the Senate does, especially about the 'advice and consent' responsibility of the Senate. We are going to see to it that they know more and that they know what we want them to know."

Senator Kilgore (R. Wyoming) asked a pointed question of the Leader, "I hate to admit ignorance, but I really don't know the technical details of what we can and can't do, and the same thing for the sitting president. I would appreciate a cogent and in-depth presentation from you, Mr. Leader."

For nearly two hours, the senators listened, took notes, and watched videos prepared by the leader and the Senate Whip depicting the process and the moral and legal correctness of what the leader was planning.

Sybil knew most of the details of the ongoing impeachment discussions being held by the bipartisan committee behind closed doors because she had a spy. That spy was one of the few real friends she had in the Senate, Republican Senator Rolf Kilgore from Cheyenne, Wyoming. The same day as the majority leader held his meeting with his senators on impedance of the president's efforts, Sen. Kilgore had an Oval Office appointment, one that was not scheduled or acknowledged.

After Sen. Kilgore read from his notes about what was being said and planned, the president asked, "So, Rolf, what is the first move?"

"They think you are ignorant of governmental processes and that you have hired a bunch of morons as staffers. Furthermore, they frankly think you are stupid, Madam President, present company excepted."

"Thank you for that, Rolf. I won't forget what you are doing for me."

"Actually, I consider it my duty. What the Senate is planning is inimitable to good government, and I am completely opposed to it.

"The first maneuver is to ignore you. To hold endless obfuscating committee meetings every time one of your appointees is introduced to the Senate, no matter that you have vetted the appointee for months and the GAO has had its process for an equally long time."

"And, they expect me to do nothing?"

"As I said, Madam President, and forgive me for saying it out loud; but they do really think you are stupid."

"Thanks for the heads up, my friend. We'll all see how this pans out over time."

Sybil really did not take much offense; she just considered the source and the spurious reasoning the Senate was employing.

Three weeks later, Sybil had submitted 150 PA [Presidentially Appointed positions] which did not require Senate approval, and even those made no progress towards navigating their way through the federal quagmire. She sent appointment requests for SAS [Senior Executive Service] and Schedule C [political] appointees, and none of them even got to sit before a Senate committee. There were 1,217 PAS positions, 789 SES positions, and 1,392 Schedule C positions all told potentially for the president to deal with; and more than thirty percent were going unfilled as a result of senatorial obstinacy. All appointments to SES and Schedule C posts had to be reviewed and approved by the Executive Office of the President; and everyone had been fully vetted, to no avail.

It was obvious to Sybil that the wheels of the government wagon were becoming weak and stiff, and she had to do something about it before the wheels fell off her wagon. She did two things: she found friendly media officials who began a news crusade to inform the public about the responsibilities of the Senate and their failure to do their sworn duty. They carefully and frequently touted the good job President Daniels was doing despite the obstacles put in her path by the vindictive Senate.

Next, she acted in her official capacity as president under the rules of the Constitution.

First, she had her staffers and her friend, Rolf Kilgore, tell her whenever a Senate recess was being called for any reason. The first recess was called because the Senate offices were being given a thorough Spring cleaning, and it was difficult to get anything done for two weeks.

By a series of Presidential Orders, Sybil pushed through the absent Senate sixty-two judgeships, twenty-seven ambassadorial positions, and another two hundred eighty-two assorted much needed PAS positions (82), SES positions (174), and Schedule C positions (622). The result was that when the senators returned from their recess, they found that a one-upmanship coup had been accomplished by the "stupid and ignorant" president. A howl went up that could be heard throughout the hallowed halls of Congress and across the nation. Majority Leader Nichols rushed to set in motion plans to thwart the president's brazen move.

Constitutional scholars unanimously agreed that the president's move was not only legal, but it was constitutional. A recess appointment under Article II, Section 2, *Clause 3*, of the Constitution, explained the attorneys and university law professors is a perfectly legal alternative method of appointing officials that allows the filling of vacancies to maintain the continuity of administrative government through the temporary filling of offices during periods when the Senate is not in session—i.e. in recess.

"However," Law Professor, Ian Tracy from Columbia University, explained to the mollification of Senate Leader

Nichols, "A recess appointment must be confirmed by the Senate by the end of the next session of Congress, or the appointment expires. In practice, this means that a recess appointment must be approved by roughly the end of the next calendar year most times.

Leader Nichols clapped his hands, "So, she can only get a temporary and short appointment over on us. Good work, Professor Tracy."

"Hold your horses, Mr. Leader, "it is not nearly so simple or easy. The way the Senate works, it could be until the end of a current senatorial term; so, it could last for almost two full years."

Leader Nichols commented angrily in language unbecoming, which reflected the general attitude of his fellow senators in the closed-door meeting.

His scholars pointed out to him about a little used maneuver that favored Congress, especially the Senate. Pro-forma meetings can be held even if no one attends which fill up the absentee period while senators are absent. Therefore, there is never a "recess"; and the president is foiled.

No sooner than the Senate instituted pro-forma meetings, the White House filed suit in the federal judicial system. The attorneys argued abuse of power and a form of fraud, since no actual work was being done. The pro-forma meetings were nothing more than a scheme to get around the intent of the Constitution. The judges ruled that: "The convening of periodic pro-forma sessions in which no business is to be conducted does not have the legal effect of interrupting an intrasession recess otherwise long enough to qualify as a "Recess of the Senate" under the Recess

Appointments Clause. In this context, the President therefore has discretion to conclude that the Senate is unavailable to perform its advise-and-consent function and to exercise his power to make recess appointments"

Sybil was once again to get a few appointments implemented when the Senate held recesses for reasons compelling to the members. That bit of empowerment for the president—however–was short lived.

Another court ruled that pro-forma meetings were adjudicated to be legal and official if both houses of Congress held such meetings throughout the now vacated "recess period". That is, the pro-forma meeting arrangement meant that Congress was in session year around; and, if the president did not like it, she could lump it.

Sybil's friends and scholars investigated to find more loopholes. They discovered that words have meaning and learned the meaning of key words for their side: "proforma" became the great obstacle; and as unfair as it seemed to the president, she got the blame for the government's failure to get her appointment requests through the gauntlet. "Recess" disappeared from the senatorial and congressional lexicon. "End-run" took on a sinister, but compelling definition so far as governing in the United States was concerned.

Sybil had a closed-door meeting with her new Chief-of-Staff, Lieutenant-general Kurt Draper, who replaced President Willet's Chief of Staff, Gen. Omar Zabriski, when he retired.

"Madam President, there are two things that have to be addressed in addition to the obvious—the situation in North Korea. Most of our time will be spent on that recurring hot spot; so, if it is all right with you, let's start with the stalemate with the Senate, then go to the need for a new vice president; then, we can get to the brinkmanship going on in Korea Bay."

CHAPTER FOUR

Sybil templed her fingers on the bridge of her nose, her usual habit when coming to a final decision. She looked Gen. Draper—her chief-of-staff--in the eye and gave him two succinct orders.

"General, have a Presidential Order prepared for my signature that declares the president's constitutional power to "convene or adjourn Congress" on this extraordinary occasion and announce my decision to exercise this constitutional prerogative--a power that has never been used until now. Announce that I hereby suspend both houses of Congress and override all pro forma procedures. In the interests of achieving a return to sensible government, I shall make appointments to vacant government positions while Congress is suspended and will continue the suspension until the Senate comes to its senses."

"Can you really do that, Madam President?" Gen. Draper asked, unable to keep the incredulity out of his voice.

"I can. It's constitutional—Article II, Section 3—and I quote: "'He shall from time to time give to the Congress information of the state of the union, and recommend to their consideration such measures as he shall judge necessary and expedient; he may, on extraordinary occasions, convene both Houses, or either of them, and in case of disagreement between them, with respect to the time of adjournment, he may adjourn them to such time as he shall think proper; he shall receive ambassadors and other public ministers; he shall take care that the laws be faithfully executed, and shall commission all the officers of the United States.' Let me underscore the key provision: 'In Case of Disagreement between [the Houses], with Respect to the Time of Adjournment, [the President] may adjourn them to such Time as he shall think proper'. At this moment in time, I deem it to be proper to do so. And, more than incidentally, put 'she' in parentheses beside every use of the word, 'he'."

Gen. Draper smiled and said, "Well, nobody can accuse you of not doing your homework. It will be interesting to see the look on the faces of the Congress and the Senate when they read this order from the woman they call, 'weak', 'ignorant', and 'stupid'. I think you ought to double your Secret Service guard units. And, I will comply as soon as our conversation is over, Ma'am."

"Now, as to the selection of a vice-president," President Daniels said, "I would appreciate it if you would quietly arrange for Senator Rolf Kilgore from Wyoming to come to the office for a chat. Bring him in from the back without fanfare."

"Aye, aye, Ma'am."

Half an hour later, the senator was sitting in the Oval Office facing the president. She got up from the desk and walked around; so, she could sit next to him.

"Okay, if I call you Rolf?"

"I'd like that, Madam President."

"I'll get right down to cases; so, you can get back to the Senate chamber without people really realizing that you were gone. You are here because I believe that you support me for the most part. Is that still true?"

"Definitely."

"I realize it's getting tougher and tougher, but I need a special favor from you. I cannot trust my own insights about individual senators, and I do trust yours. You can't help but be aware that I need to appoint a successor vice-president, and I need to do it pronto."

Sen. Kilgore gulped, and he looked crestfallen.

Sybil laughed, "No, Rolf, I would not wish that useless job on you. We are friends. Here is what I want you to do. Get me a short list of half a dozen or less potential candidates. Surely, there are that many who are not 'never Danielses'; and ones that have decent reputations, no skeletons in their closets or freezers; and, most important, a man or woman who could conceivably be president in case I die or am removed."

"Madam President, you are not as unpopular in the Senate as you might think. Your history as a neurosurgeon, as DCIA, as the surgeon general, and as the vice-president, has won you real admirers. They don't speak up, but there are a reasonable number who actually approve of how your list of more than your share of huge problems is being handled. I will have you a list before quitting time today."

"Thank you, Rolf. You have my marker. I won't forget."

Lt. Gen. Draper waited until Sen. Kilgore left the Oval Office.

"Madam President. We need to talk about the unpleasantness going on in Korea Bay. Would you like me to get the DirNSA to join us?"

"Yes, and for now, let's keep it among the three of us."

Draper pushed a button on his iPhone and was rewarded almost instantly by the voice of Lt. Gen. Robert Wayne Reynolds, the DIRNSA [Director of the National Security Agency].

"Yes, General? I am on a secure line."

"Come to the Oval Office now."

"Yes, Sir. I'm right down the hall."

Two minutes later the president, the DIRNSA, and the chief-of-staff began their conversation about the North Korean bellicosity, intransigence, and potential for further serious mischief.

In response to Sybil's open-ended query, Reynolds said, "We have our three carrier strike force groups--the USS Nimitz, the USS Reagan, and the USS Theodore Roosevelt in place off the coast of the DPRK in international waters. They are ready to commence action if ordered or if fired upon. LTG Bills, commander of the Eighth Army and Gen. Robert Abrams, commander of the United Nations Command, Combined Forces Command and United States Forces Korea are at DEFCON 2. We are ready for a short-term war; and, if all hell breaks out, we can triple our presence within a day and a half."

"Good. Have you heard from anyone from the DPRK?"

"Yes, we have a kind of back channel and only quasi-official communication. The man says he is Lt. Qwan Ling Ho, and that he is acting under Dear Leader Kim's orders to convey messages back and forth. Nothing newsworthy coming from him so far."

"That's about as low a man on the totem pole as they could round up, unless we were treated to negotiations with people's lead street sweeper for Pyongyang," Sybil said ruefully.

"Do you think this Lt. Qwan will talk to me?"

"Who knows? Even if he does, it's anybody's guess as to whether or not the message will actually reach Kim Jong Un; and if he does get it, will he communicate back; or if he does communicate back whether or not he will negotiate in good faith?"

"That triple negative scenario is likely and would simplify things. I am in no mood to negotiate, and I certainly will not submit to blackmail," President Daniels with a level of determination that made Lt. Gen. Reynolds glad that she was the commander-in-chief for the time being.

"I'll see if I can get him to talk to you, Ma'am."

"Well, General, you know where to get hold of me; I'm pretty much always at home."

CHAPTER FIVE

President Daniels's Presidential Order for mandatory adjournment of the Congress came to the Speaker and the Majority Leader at precisely the same time—7:00 p.m. on Friday. To put salt in their wounds, Sybil had arranged for the message to be delivered by courier to each leader's private home. It was too late for the message to get out to the supper time viewers, at too poor a time for a large number of late evening viewers to catch it, and arrived at a carefully chosen moment when the majority of members of the Congress had left for recess—or were getting feedback from their pro-forma group meetings attended by two groups of one. Saturday and Sunday are traditionally dead days for news, and this weekend was no exception.

Speaker Zimbrowski was apoplectic. Majority Leader Nichols had to be taken to Walter Reed for observation because of chest pain. President Daniels had a great and cathartic laugh when she learned there was a four-hour electrical failure in the exclusive Kalorama neighborhood of the District of Columbia where the speaker and the majority leader lived. Everybody who is anybody in the nation's capital lives in that neighborhood, situated north of Dupont Circle. It is an historic neighborhood which has become home to numerous illuminati in media, politics, diplomacy, lobbying, and big business. Sybil shed copious crocodile tears knowing that Speaker Zimbrowski and Leader Nichols lived there and there would be great frustration for the two movers and shakers to communicate with news media confrères.

Monday morning did come as it inevitably had to. The two congressional leaders demanded an Oval Office meeting with the president. Sybil's secretary, Mrs. Carpentier, sweetly informed them that the first opening in the president's extremely busy schedule would be five minutes at the end of the day Thursday. Both the lady and the gentlemen used language unbecoming to members of polite society to describe their displeasure. Mabel Carpentier–a devote Methodist–considered that being subjected to such language did not fit into her job description; and she was horrified. She peremptorily hung up on them.

Sixteen members of the House of Representatives and twelve senators gathered in Speaker Zimbrowski's house in the Kalorama neighborhood and worked through the day to draft an appeal for an immediate injunction by the Supreme Court. The court clerk informed the angry senator who delivered the request that it had to go through a federal district court first; it was protocol. Fuming, Senator Leesdale got back in his limo and was taken to the United States District Court, Greenbelt Division courthouse on 6500 Cherrywood Lane in Greenbelt. It was nine-thirty in the morning, and Senator Leesdale learned that the court secretary was on an errand for Judge Clinton and would not be back for an hour. His harangue against the student intern who was fielding questions only made her cry. When she informed the secretary—her boss—Ingrid Haufstedder, Ms. Haufstedder suddenly learned of a second errand that added an additional hour to her absence from the courthouse.

Senator Leesdale literally screamed. The intern cried uncontrollably; and finally, the senator stomped out of the building. Two hours later, he returned—somewhat calmed by a couple of stiff drinks that he referred to as "Tee martoonies" in a giggle—with three additional, more senior, more sober, but just as angry senators, to the courthouse to find a long line waiting in the lobby to see the formidable Ms. Haufstedder.

Republican Senator Pinkton of New York marched through the long line of waiting people and shouted his demands to be seen first—because he was the senior senator from New York. A degree of animosity developed on the part of the people who had been patiently enduring a long wait. Senator Pinkton responded in kind, and finally court security guards were summoned to sort things out. The senator was determined to have been at fault and had actually thrown a punch. The receiver of his punch was a burly border patrol doing his duty for the bureau. He decked the senator. He was found to have acted in self-defense and was allowed to stay. The senator was roughly escorted to the courthouse steps holding a law enforcement citation to meet a growing crowd of reporters who mysteriously showed up at just that time.

Acting on orders from the chief judge, the court officers closed the courthouse doors to allow the people who had been waiting such a long time to see Ms. Haufstedder, to remain; but the closure barred the doors to anyone who had arrived later, including three very angry senators. It was nearly two in the afternoon before the waiting people were served, and the chief judge closed the court to anything but courts in session for the rest of the day to allow things to calm down.

It was not until ten the next morning that two humble senate clerks, both eighteen years old, were seen by Ms. Haufstedder.

"Gentlemen, I realize that you are just messengers, but it is my duty to tell you that the request for an injunction directed to the supreme court will have to be re-written to conform with protocol. First, the injunction will have to be directed to the United States District Court; then, when the chief judge agrees with the validity of the request, he will have one of his secretaries find a place on the docket of one of the seven judges."

The clerks–being the messengers–were not shot when they arrived back at the Hart Senate Office Building with their bad news. But, they were excoriated by four extremely angry senators. The following morning, three experienced and hardened attorneys took the newly minted injunction papers back to Ms. Haufstedder's lobby, waited their turn, and were politely directed to the chief judge's office.

A pleasantly plump bespecaled young secretary sweetly told the attorneys, "I will be happy to help you, Gentlemen...let's see...no not on Thursday...oh, yes,

Judge Franklin's secretary can see you and make an appointment for you to be heard in his court."

"And how long might that be, please," the eldest of the senate attorneys asked in his best syrupy sweet honeyed voice.

There was a pause as the obliging secretary thumbed through a stack of papers.

"About a month," she said with a pleasant smile.

The senatorial attorneys left almost empty handed and gave written reports, not wanting to have to endure facing the wrathful senators.

Ms. Haufstedder had lunch with Mrs. Carpentier the following day and confided confidentally the story of the injunction's travels. Ms. Haufstedder was an ardent feminist, and a fan of President Daniels; so, she might have embellished a bit.

When Mrs. Carpentier reported back to the president, she and her chief of staff had to sit on a sofa to enjoy their long and refreshing laugh.

Of course, the networks got wind of the president having officially adjourned Congress, and the news outlets had a field day. There was almost nothing else but news of the adjournment and scads of commercials on CNN, Fox News, CBS, NBC, MSNBC, and ABC, for three full days. Somehow, the fiasco at the Greenbelt Courthouse, came to light and added a touch of levity to the "Breaking News" for an additional two days.

President Daniels enjoyed her short break from the seemingly endless attacks being made on her and her administration.

However, the clouds of wars and rumors of wars began to close in again. The focus of attention was now in Korea Bay where a small squadron of North Korean naval vessels began making feints and short forays aimed at the carrier *Theodore Roosevelt*. Because the carrier and its associated vessels did not fire, the officers on the small vessels of the KPN [*Chosŏn'gŭl*-Korean People's Army Naval Force] were emboldened by their mistaken impression that the Americans were paper tigers.

Adm. Trescott, on board the *Theodore Roosevelt*, fretted that the KPN braggarts would make a mistake.

"What do we do if one of those monkeys on a guided-missile patrol boats trips over a rope and accidently fires off an errant SS-N-2A STYX antiship missile? he asked rhetorically.

"Heaven, forbid," the XO, Capt. Leander Fife said with a shudder.

Almost before Capt. Fife could finish his sentence, an overly excited *Sanggŭp-pyŏngsa* [US equivalent, Petty Officer First Class] accidentally flipped a switch and launched a torpedo. The trajectory of the torpedo was significantly off course from the *Theodore Roosevelt* and headed into international waters.

Capt. Fife piped an order to the weapons room, "Kill it."

A very satisfying explosion occurred four nauts off the port side.

"Good shot," observed Adm. Trescott. "As I interpret our orders, we have been fired upon. Take out the guided missile patrol boat."

The crew of the North Korean boat had been watching with horrified fascination as its accidental torpedo launch wobbled its way to destruction. They did not have to wonder long what the paper tigers were going to do. In a blinding instant of smoke, fire, metal debris, and dismembered body parts, the boat disappeared beneath the otherwise calm sea.

In Pyongyang and Washington, admirals and politicians held their breaths, wondering if the die had been cast to start World War III.

President Daniels was summoned to the Situation Room and apprised of the incident by General Glen Gabler, Sr. the CJCS. He neither embellished nor diminished the incident; it was what it was.

The CNO, Admiral Robert Gillespie, asked, "Madam President. It's your call; should we push forward, back off, apologize, or threaten. Should I recall Admiral Trescott and reprimand him as part of an apology?"

President Daniels shook her head, "Too many options. I will start with the last first. No reprimand. He stays, and maybe he and his ship should get medals. However, I am not quite ready to launch thermonuclear war. I am going to give one more try to get Kim Jong Un, the Dear Leader to talk to me and maybe to listen to reason. Stand in place for now."

Adm. Gillespie said, "Thank you, Madam President. I would have resigned before I issued a reprimand. You know, The North Korean navy is considered everywhere to be a brown water navy and operates almost entirely within the 50 kilometer exclusion zone. It is more likely than not that little will happen while you get to exercise a little diplomacy."

CHAPTER SIX

Sybil did not have time—not even a few minutes—to deal with the irate congresspersons and senators. She actually wanted to confront them head on to clear the air and to begin working towards solutions to the nation's serious problems. However, the issue of North Korea now loomed front and center.

Secretary of State Fiona Del Giordia and her staff had been on their lines making every possible attempt to get Chairman Kim or almost any senior DPRK officer to communicate. Secy. Del Giordia finally was able to get hold of the senior member of the Swiss legation—Ferdinand Delasse--who had been handling what few affairs the United States had with North Korea.

"Ferdinand, I know you're busy," she started, "but we have a situation with our nice friends in the north of the Korean Peninsula which has a real potential to conflagrate and soon. We need your help today."

"Give me the background, please, Fiona."

She did and emphasized the critical need to get President Daniels and Chairman Kim together by phone.

"It is an opportune time, even this very day," Ferdinand said, "Deputy Chairman Lee contacted me less than an hour ago. He demanded that I get the 'crazy Americans'—his words, not mine—to talk with his Dear Leader. He acknowledged grudgingly that the DPRK's communications system had been experiencing a series of rolling brownouts which have been frustrating; but they have not wanted to admit to that, as you can well imagine. If you can hang on the line for a little while, I think I can get through to Kim on a line maintained by a generator. He won't admit to the generator either. I think some heads are about to roll up there."

It did take a while, a fairly long while. Ferdinand first had to call the North Korean embassy in Bern. He was told that Bern would transfer the call to the Swiss embassy in Beijing. Beijing accepted the call—this being the usual route the Swiss legation had to follow—and made the antepenultimate call to the Swiss cooperation office in the Taedonggang River District of Pyongyang. The cooperation office placed a priority call to Dear Leader's private residence and office Ryongsong Residence Residence [also called Residence No. 55 and popularly known by locals as Central Luxury Mansion].

"This is Kim Han Jin from the Taedonggang River Swiss office. I am passing a call to our Dear and Precious Leader from the United States Secretary of State and her president."

Kim is a very common name in North Korea; however, Kim Han Jin was the Dear Leader's cousin; and, therefore, his name carried real weight.

"Immediately, Sir. I most honored to transmit your call, Mr. Kim."

Three secretaries later, the Supreme Leader of North Korea and chairman of the Workers' Party of Korea came on the line. Without hesitation, he agreed to answer the call, so long as the president of the United States guaranteed to be on the line once the required routing was accomplished.

The routing then reversed directions until it finally came to rest again in the office of Ferdinand Delasse. After confirming that he was who he said he was, Ferdinand was permitted to hand the phone to Secy. Del Giordia.

"Mr. Chairman, this is Fiona del Giordia, Secretary of State for the United States. Thank you for accepting my call."

"I prefer to have you use my title as Supreme Leader or Dear Leader, as our loving people call me."

"Of course, Dear Leader. I am acting for the president who would like to speak to you about concerns the United States has with the Democratic People's Republic of Korea."

"It will be good for us to speak," Chairman Kim said, "make it happen."

Her assistant was already getting through the formalities of security in order to connect with President Daniels. She came on in less than three minutes.

"Dear Leader," she said, "I am sorry you had to wait so long on the line."

She mimed sticking her finger down her throat, glad that they were not on facetime.

"No problem, my dear friend, Sybil. Do you mind if I call you Sybil? It seems that we can accomplish more as friends, don't you think?"

"Of course, Dear Leader."

"Oh, Sybil, you can just call me Mr. Kim."

"Thank you, Mr. Kim. I know how busy you are, and I will not waste your precious time. As I am sure you are aware, an unfortunate incident occurred in Korea Bay this morning. My fellow Americans and I are concerned that this can escalate, which would be a most unfortunate thing. I seek your opinion and directions about how we might proceed."

Another gagging mime.

"It is only fair that you compensate our navy for the destruction of the ship and the families of the ship's crew for their tragic losses. The grief and pain of the dear people of our small country would be further improved by a generous contribution such as money for construction of a memorial and for a highway leading out of Pyongyang to the memorial and from there to Huichon. I will order my people to accept this paltry token from your country."

Sybil again mimed a gagging gesture, but this time, her jaws became clenched in what her friends recognized as her demonstration that she had reached the end of her patience and tether.

"Mr. Chairman, you perhaps have forgotten to whom you are speaking. I am not the 'paper tiger' your press says of me. I am the president of the United States, and neither I nor my country will be bullied or extorted. You will cease and desist from these ongoing provocations, or you will suffer the consequences. Unlike most of my predecessors, I do not believe in shows of force or half-way measures. If you launch even one more attack, we will remove you and your little country from the planet.

"My most important obligation, and one that I have sworn to obey, is the protection of all Americans. I will not allow even one American to be wounded or killed on my watch. Not even one. An attack on one is an attack on us all. Stand down, Sir, or see destruction beyond your imagination. Ask Beijing about me; do I exaggerate?"

The Dear Leader was fuming at such affrontery, and he began a shouting diatribe in reply, "My country is not without excellent defenses, not without good friends, and not without resolve. Your tyrannical country will regret the day you first fire on us."

He listened for a response, then for breathing. Then, he realized that he had been cut off.

Sybil informed the joint chiefs and the Congress of her conversation with Chairman Kim. During her brief conversation with Majority Leader Nichols, she invited him and the Speaker and their top aides to a small informal noon luncheon in the Jackie Kennedy Garden located on the east side of the South Portico. He accepted for his congressional counterpart.

The Secret Service hurried into action to provide security for the event. They were not at all fond of such open venues, but it was hardly the first time they had had to do the same job. They were ready by noon. Sybil's personal guard unit—she knew all their names and called them by their Christian names—reconnoitered the White House grounds, the entryways, the surrounding roadways, and the roof. All traffic going any direction was halted during the activity.

Gordon Langtree--President Daniels's chief Secret Service security guard--had a strong reputation for thoroughness and for being detail minded—some felt, to a fault. He walked to the roof of the White House to inspect the protective units there. Special Agent Steven Nilsson greeted him without rising; so, he could avoid revealing his position to any onlookers. He and Langtree were both GS-13s. Nilsson's special tracks had been language (he spoke three fluently) and marksmanship. Before being recruited for the Secret Service he had been a marine sniper.

Langtree had a near photographic memory which led to his reputation for ferreting out and remembering details. Their skills were a good match.

The two men sat and watched for their drone to pass overhead sending out real time images of the grounds, entryways, and foliage, with emphasis on the Kennedy Garden. Langtree took a last look at the area through Nilsson's high-powered binoculars before making his declaration. He also took note of the obviously well-maintained Wilson Combat AR-10 Recon Tactical sniper rifle with a clean matte black barrel. He knew it held twenty rounds, 21 if a chambered round was in place.

"Looks fine to me," he said. "Here are photographs of every special agent on duty today and pix of the bad guys who keep saying nasty stuff about the president and making themselves too visible and prominent around the White House and at the president's activities. Keep a high level of suspicion, My Friend."

"Always do."

Sybil Norcroft's reputation for punctuality inspired her guests to arrive shortly before noon; so, they wouldn't commit the gaucherie of tardiness—a moral failure of which the president took note.

There were twenty guests and their wives, ten secret service special agents, and Sybil and Charles Daniels present and accounted for. Sybil was all smiles and geniality when she strode informally up to the small podium set up close to the White House building. She intended to give a few light remarks and then to move a little closer to the pesky issues separating her and her legislative "colleagues".

"Friends and neighbors, I hope everyone here enjoys Chef Louis's special picnic. He has worked to outdo himself. I won't spend long speechifying…

A shot from a high-powered rifle rang out and passed close enough to singe Sybil's shining blond hair as it missed her head. Pandemonium ensued. Secret Service agents fell upon Sybil and Charles, momentarily pinning them to the ground. More arrived and formed a protective cordon around them to get them back into the building. A large force of agents descended into the garden and swiftly pulled the important guests to safety. What looked chaotic was actually a well-practiced drill, and no one was hurt.

CHAPTER SEVEN

A twenty-block cordon was thrown up around the White House in a matter of minutes by the US Secret Service, FBI, US Marshalls Service, US National Parks Federal Police, US Capitol Police, Metropolitan Police Department of the District of Columbia, and the District of Columbia Protective Services Division. The issue was clear—find the would-be killer of the president and do it now—so, there was no squabbling over turf or jurisdiction.

Citizens rushed to get their parked cars off the streets and then stayed inside their homes. Rush hour moved with glacial celerity because every vehicle going out of DC was subjected to serious scrutiny, and helicopters by the dozens buzzed the mall and around the streets running into and out of the area of the Capitol and the Hill. Thousands of people were questioned, and their smart phones were scoured.

Following protocol Special Agent Steven Nilsson remained in place atop the White House in his sniper perch looking, squinting, binocularing, and checking feed from the drone. It would have been boring except for the fact that his attention was fully focused on his job. Find the shooter. Find anything that was moving that should not be moving or had the shape of a human. His eyes were burning and weary. He had to fight not only drowsiness but the tendency to see things move that were inanimate. The biggest excitement thus far was a pair of squirrels that raced across the Kennedy Garden lawn.

Inside the Situation Room, President Daniels was getting input from dozens of sources via dozens of electronic resources. Special Agents of the FBI questioned the president and Charles in exquisite and annoying detail about any enemies they had. There were so many for President Daniels that the agents stopped even writing them down. No one really popped out. Everyone in the country knew that there was an established hate-hate relationship between her and the congressional leaders, but no law enforcement officer gave any credence to a conspiracy involving the Speaker, the Majority Leader, and the president.

Special Agent Owen Matthews said out loud what most officers were thinking.

"I'm thinking that the 500-pound gorilla in the room is that 5'9" little Rocket Man in North Korea. Everyone I talk to says he would be nuts to pull a stunt like this. He has to know that our President would be sifting through his ashes a few minutes after we prove that he ordered it. Is he nuts? Is he ready for a war? or is he just very crafty and a man with very capable spies and saboteurs?"

The DNI and DCIA agreed that it was hypothetically possible, but there was not a scintilla of evidence to support SA Matthews's hypothesis. The FBI was rapidly rounding up all the loonies, conspirators, and Islamic radicals, in a three-state area and grilling them.

Secret Service Special Agent Nilsson had been sitting and fidgeting in his snipers' next for a full two days, and he was hungry. His hunch had not paid off he guessed, and any more persistence was not required by the secret service presidential protection protocol any longer. He stretched out his aching knees and arched his back. Just to satisfy his inner need, he took one more look at the trees surrounding the Kennedy Garden through his binoculars. He saw a fellow agent striding purposefully across the lawn away from the White House and towards the dense trees on the opposite side.

Then, all his senses came alive. A bush moved. It was no illusion. It was still moving. In a moment he could make out two brushy legs and two vine covered arms. He was looking at the best ghillie suit he had ever laid eyes on. The bushiness was accurate in every detail to the foliage in that section of trees, bushes, and grasses. This was the sniper. He had on a camouflaged heavy steel helmet, and this sniper had a long rifle slung over his shoulder. From his perch on the White House roof, Nilsson could clearly make out the moment that the secret service agent and the man in the ghillie suit locked eyes on each other. The special agent appeared not to be sure what he was seeing. He shook his head.

The hit man shrugged his shoulder, and the cruel looking rifle was falling into a shooting position. The ghillie suited man dropped to one knee and took aim.

The agent on the lawn was moving in what looked to Nilsson like he was sleep walking or had wooden arms and legs. He was a dead man.

Except…secret service agent/sniper/fully alert and functional marksman fired off one round in the quarter second before the would-be killer got his shot off. The man in the ghillie suit took a 6.5 Creedmore round to the top of his head, and everything above his nose disappeared in a fireball explosion. He was on the White House lawn dead before the secret service agent in the Kennedy Garden could process the fact that he had been saved.

The fireball explosion came from Nilsson's special ammunition: 6.5 caliber Creedmore bullet with HEIAP [high-explosive-incendiary filling armor-piercing ammunition]. The round was a specially made tungsten alloy bullet with a tungsten carbide penetrator. This developed a very large amount of kinetic energy able to penetrate armor like a hardened steel helmet just as a solid-cored armor-piercing shot would be expected to do. in addition, the extra kinetic energy propelled on the incendiary material and its twenty steel fragments--created by the explosives—and delivered them in a 25–30 degree cone through the armor followed by an explosion more than adequate to remove a man's head, and to top it all off, an intensely hot, long burning, fire increased lethality—the very definition of overkill. Nilsson had not given even a first thought about winging the man.

The autopsy on the sniper was inconclusive, with the lack of information being quite remarkable. He was a white male, age 30-35, average height, build, and weight. No scars, tattoos, or other markings, and no jewelry. Attempts at obtaining facial recognition on the FBI data base revealed almost negligible results—his face had been blown and burned away. Expedited DNA samples revealed that he was a Caucasian male of eastern European extraction, mostly from Eastern Germany and Hungary. He had no markers of heritable disease or currently unexpressed syndromes.

FBI investigation of his clothing was similarly unproductive: after canvassing dozens of cheap clothing stores, it was determined that his shirt, pants, socks, and underclothing, had most probably been purchased in an army-navy surplus store called the Army Ten-Miler on 102 3rd Avenue in the district the previous week--a store that had a nonfunctioning cheap U60VW video camera surveillance system. No one remembered anyone making a specific purchase of one of the cheapest and most commonly sold outfits. No sniper rifles or ghillie suits had been sold in months, and careful examination of the suit in question revealed that it had been handmade by a nonprofessional–but highly experienced–camouflage maker. The staff of the store did not know of any outlet in the city that made such suits. In short, the investigators drew a blank.

FBI investigators examined the bureau's extensive data base on ballistics and rifles and determined that the ammunition had been homemade and was untraceable. The rifle itself was a fairly commonly purchased item for long-distance shooting enthusiasts. They interviewed 482 owners—all living—and all in possession of their rifles. No joy there.

Once again, the Speaker of the House, and the Majority Leader of the Senate, requested a meeting with President Daniels. She was leery; she sighed; but she guessed she was sufficiently over the scare of her life to meet her avowed enemies one more time. She wondered out loud in the privacy of the Oval Office what in the world they wanted this time.

Mrs. Carpentier showed the two congressional leaders in.

"Welcome," Sybil said and made it seem sincere.

"Thank you for seeing us today, of all days," the speaker said. "We come bearing an olive branch."

Sybil raised one eyebrow.

"For real," the leader said. "Look, for all of our disagreement with you; we still acknowledge that you are the president…our president; and we are patriotic Americans whatever conclusions you may have drawn otherwise. We want to achieve a truce among us…not just a truce, but a real peace."

"Like working together instead of at odds with each other?" Sybil queried.

"Yes, Madam President, just like that. We held serious discussions in both of our houses, and there was near unanimity that we Americans must close ranks. Several senators—especially the senator from Wyoming—pointed out that our fight was actually just a disagreement over what the Constitution means and neither of our branches had personal issues or truly believed that you were defying us out of some sort of personal animus or ambition.

Senator Rolf Kilgore put it most convincingly: 'we have enemies from without and within, and now was no time for us to go about tearing the country apart.' We ask you to work with us and to allow us to work with you to solve our nation's problems," Leader Nichols said, and it was entirely evident that he meant every word.

"I'm surprised and pleased," Madam Speaker and Mister Majority Leader. "How do you propose that we proceed?"

It was asked honestly and taken at face value by her erstwhile opponents.

"Probably the place to begin is to put all our energy into finding the criminals who ordered the hit on you, Sybil," Majority Leader Nichols said. "Pardon me for being personal and presumptive by using your Christian name, but I feel deeply personal about all of this."

"I do too, of course; so, in this room, let us be Sybil, Shirley, and Ralph."

The speaker said, "My friends call me Shirl. Would that be okay?"

Sybil shined her patented and not often used smile and said, "Shirl it is."

"Can you tell us how the investigation is going, Sybil," Shirl asked.

Sybil said, "Let's jump to the end. The answer right now is 'nowhere'. It is definitely a work in progress. That being true, my suggestion is to let the FBI do their work; and let us somewhat divide up the crucial problems and start working on them. As soon as we separate, I will rescind my order of adjournment of the Congress and count on you to process my appointment requests in a regular fashion."

"Agreed."

"My most pressing issue at the very moment is the belligerency of North Korea. Let me devote my full attention on that. Shirl, you have the most widespread influence; so, maybe you can deal with the Gordian Knot of the infrastructure repair; and Ralph, would it work for you to take the lead in getting the House and the Senate on track to get the rest of the legislative issues on a forward track. From the executive, I promise no stumbling blocks. You can work through the White House Liaison. Shirl, I will get the cabinet on board. You can work with Treasury, Labor, and Commerce, or anyone else you need. That ought to get us through the day, don't you think?"

"And tomorrow, we can accomplish world peace, abolishment of hunger, abuse of women and children, and poverty," said Ralph, and the new friends enjoyed a communal relieving laugh.

CHAPTER EIGHT

Freed of the entanglements and time expenditure of the congressional battles, worry about impeachment, and the struggles to get her grand hope of repairing the infrastructure of the United States, Sybil set about to deal with the unfinished business of North Korean belligerency and obstinacy. She hoped to deal, or at least start to deal with two problems at once.

She contacted the ODNI to arrange an ultra-secret communication with the Prime Minister of the United Kingdom, Lord Blancomb. The apparatus to make the connection was not quite as smooth in the UK for communication since the tenure of Benjamin Wood-Jackson and his belligerent populists.

The overseas secure line operator announced to President Daniels, "Prime Minister Lord Blancomb is on the line now, Madam President."

"Hello, David," she greeted him.

"Oh, good, now its back to 'David'. I presume the ultra-secret communication is something more than a well-wish, Sybil."

"It some of both, My Friend. I am sure you have been following the progress of my tenure in office. You must think that I have somehow offended God or that I have the worst luck of any world leader since Ben Wood-Jackson."

"Well, I prefer the 'God' angle to the 'Wood-Jackson' one, which is a bit on my part since I am a confirmed atheist. You never heard that from me. Now, what can I do for you?"

"David, we can do for each other. I'll bring you up to date on my situation…situations, then we can discuss our mutual needs and benefits."

"Sounds like a plan to me."

Sybil told him about the events of the previous day and a half which caused him to inhale a breath of incredulity.

"But," she said, "things in my realm are getting back to the train being on the tracks for a change, and you and I can talk about things going on between our two countries. First of all, let me thank you for the first installment in reparations payments. That calmed the anger of most of the nay-sayers; and, given more recent developments, England and its money is on the back-burner. I need a favor, and I have an olive branch to offer—something of a *quid pro quo.*"

"Oh, I like it when you let drop a little Latin to demonstrate your superior private school education, Sybil."

"You should talk, Mr. Scholar with the sterling background of snooty nose-up Eton College until age 17, then two years at Dulwich College—founded in 1619, no less—followed by Cambridge University PhD in political science. Talk about hobnobbin' with the snootin' groupers."

"Touché," Lord Blancomb laughed, and Sybil shared the implicit camaraderie.

"Sorry I interrupted."

"So, back to business. Much as I would like to make a public display of forgiving the debt and letting bygones be bygones, I can't. What I can do, is ask that you skip the next payment, then send a half-payment to the treasury. After that, we can let things slide, at least as long as I am president. No telling what another populist would wreak in my place."

"Perish forbid."

"Indeed. That much I can do, much like the allies finally just forgot about reparations from Germany once the world's economies righted themselves in the post war period. I do have something to ask of you. Not really in return as a quid pro quo; the reparations offer stands alone if you don't think you can do what I'm about to ask."

"Don't keep me in suspense, Sybil. What is this big ask?"

"Let me explain my reasoning, and it will become clear. I have a couple of absolutes: the first is that I will not allow any American or British casualties if it is at all possible to accomplish that miracle. Second, I have come to believe that we can make a definitive, but small pre-emptive strike in North Korea to shatter their arrogance and bravado. Failure of that, will inevitably result in me unleashing a nuclear holocaust on the nasty little country. My reasoning, and therefore my plan, is to send our best of the best commandoes in to do a little wet work."

"There must be something wrong with me, but that sounds eminently reasonable."

"Specifically, I need a squad of your SAS black-ops people to link up with an already chosen unit from the SAC/SOG [Special Activities Center's Special Operations Group] made up largely of former elite DOD special forces types who were inveigled into joining the CIA and who have been cross-trained as regular Operations Officers. I happen to be quite well informed on this particular unit."

"I can just bet. That is something I can certainly arrange. When do you expect action?"

"They'll have to train together and try to get along with each other. We will set up a special training location at The Farm in Virginia. How much actually gets implemented depends on what Comrade Kim does in the next little while."

"I'll make my people available by the close of work today, Sybil. Thanks for asking for cooperation; it means a lot given our recent unpleasant interactions. It is good to be back to Sybil and David."

"Indeed."

As if to add punctuation to the talk with Lord Blancomb, Kim Jong Un arranged for his KCNA [Korean Central News Agency] to send a series of television videos and newspaper articles around the civilized world. The first video was shared with CNN, Fox News, ABC, NBC, and CBS. The narrator, as a prologue to the world's opportunity to hear from the Dear Leader announced:

"We are about to hear from the world's foremost leader and governmental genius. His prowess is legendary. He learned to walk when he was three weeks old and without instruction. He just observed his great father, Kim Jong Il walk about while greeting world leaders. It is known that Kim Jong Il controlled the weather, and his glorious son, our Dear Leader Kim Jong Un, controls nature. The great success of our farm system–developed by the Dear Supreme Leader–is the evidence of that power.

"You are no doubt aware of the magnificent *Meoseumnal* Festival for servants designed, planned, and carried out, by the genius of the Dear Leader whom you will hear from in today's broadcast. The singing and dancing--all written and choreographed by the Supreme Leader--was considered the most spectacular in the history of such events. It was attended by the highest dignitaries from all over the world.

"Now, it is my great honor, pleasure, and privilege, to say his name in introduction for today's great broad-cast…Kim Jong Un, our Dear, Kind, Brilliant, Supreme Leader who is worshipped by all his countrymen!"

The scene shifted to what was by now a familiar setting for Chairman Kim—his palatial office with him seated at his desk with a large flag of the DPRK draped behind him. Lights were trained on him and the flag exclusively. No microphones were in sight, but the sound was clear and precise. His English was perfect, although not always exactly in synchrony with the movements of his lips.

"Good evening, ladies and gentlemen of the world. It has become necessary for me to address all of you. I report multiple unprovoked military attacks against our strong nation which were easily rebuffed, thanks to my military preparations and decisions. These assaults are becoming too much for us to bear; they are insults even though they were committed by poorly trained weaklings and morons. We will no longer sit idly by and allow them to continue.

""America and her criminal president are responsible along with our eternal enemies, the Japanese, and the so-called South Koreans. Now they shall pay. Keep your television sets tuned in to see our retaliation unfold. In the next two weeks, you shall see a reminder of our wrath and our power. On the American holiday held on the Fourth of July by the American's incorrect calendar—you will learn to your horror—about an altogether new and most deadly strategic weapon. You will see shocking actual action. And, just to let you know from the Supreme Leader himself, we are now fully nuclear capable despite every effort by America and its spit licking lackies to impede our progress. Know that we are coming."

The scene shifted back to the attractive Korean girl who finished the program by saying, "And that concludes our program tonight. We have been honored to hear from our divine Dear Leader. He has spoken truth to power and has told the aggressors that their time shall shortly come to an end."

She gave a sweet smile, and the scene faded to dark.

The DNI said, "We know the address by Kim was pre-recorded at a four-day meeting of the Workers' Party in Pyongyang. We also have him on tape vowing that "Our country will never give up its security for economic benefits as we–the chosen people–face increasing US hostility and verified nuclear threats."

President Daniels said, "Sounds like real threats to me. My jiu jitsu instructor used to tell me never to make threats you do not intend to carry through. Action trumps bologna every time. I believe it is time to reply to the little man—excuse me, the Dear Little Man."

Sybil waited until evening in London to call Lord Blancomb again. It was brief and to the point.

"David, I presume you saw the Dear Leader's broadcast. It is time to begin calling his bluff and bluster. Please have the SAS commandoes ready to fly out tomorrow morning. Our people will be waiting at The Farm for them."

"I am ever at your disposal. Wish our teams success, My Friend."

A bomb went off in London the following day. It was crude and did little damage, and no one was killed. There had been no attempt to disguise the origin of the bomb. It had North Korean lettering on the casing fragments and a signature fuse employed by a well-known North Korean terrorist. It was them all right, and that set in stone the plans of the president and prime minister to deliver an unforgettable message.

Three weeks later, the PM and President spent an afternoon at The Farm reviewing the readiness of the SAS [Special Air Service] and the SAC/SOG unit. The CIA had hastily built a flimsy 1/10 scale model of the *Ryongsong* Residence, also called Residence No. 55 and known by locals as Central Luxury Mansion—a title never spoken out loud] which is a presidential palace in North Korea and the main residence of leader Kim Jong-un. The complex model included details obtained by CIA spies that the compound has an underground wartime headquarters, protected with walls with iron rods and concrete covered with lead in case of a nuclear war.

Numerous military units protect the headquarters stationed around the complex in possession of mass scale conventional weapons. The area is surrounded by an electric fence, mine fields, and many security check-points. The headquarters model showed the connections to *Changgyong* Residence [Residence No. 26] and several other residences by reinforced tunnels. A private underground train station is also inside the actual residence compound, and the CIA engineers constructed an accurate miniature for the black-ops agents to study.

The agents performed drills of the actual planned operation three times for the two national leaders. Each time they went through the drill it was quick, efficient, and seemed altogether plausible.

PM Blancomb asked a pointed question: "How do you get into the palace past all the security measures?"

The lead special agent—no names were given—said, "Spies, actors, liars, linguists, and blueprints. Your spies have done a marvelous job, and more than one paid with his or her life. We have agents going with us who defected years ago, still speak the dialect, and who hate the regime far more than we do. They are willing to die for this mission."

Sybil said, "I don't want them to die for this mission. I want the other guys to die for this mission."

The lead agent said with determination, "So do we, Madam President; most certainly, so do we."

A late afternoon thermite bomb set a department store on fire in Koreatown--a 15 minute drive west of DC in Annandale, Virginia. Because more than twenty-five percent of Annandale residents are of Asian descent, and the majority of them being Korean—well over 94,000 people--central Annandale is known by everyone as Koreatown. Adjacent to the store were a bakery, cyber-café, and a hair salon. The fire department crews could not get close enough to the fire to extinguish it quickly because of the intense heat generated by the thermite; so, all four businesses burned to the ground.

Sybil learned of the conflagration from the morning news, and instantly made the connection—probably the connection the North Koreans wanted her to make.

She contacted the Annandale fire department and learned that it was—as everybody expected—arson. The focal point of the origin of the fire was in a basement trash collection area, and the evidence indicated that it was a very simple device—a large lump of thermite suspended above a bucket of gasoline connected to a fuse which was activated by a cheap disposable cell phone. There was not enough left of the device to identify any Korean writing or signature manufacture indicative of a North Korea origin. The Annandale police informed Sybil that no one had seen anything suspicious. There were thousands of people of Korean extraction in and out of the department store that day. The investigation was a dead end.

"That is the last straw," Sybil said to General Glen Gabler, Sr. the CJCS, when she summoned him to the Oval Office. "Proceed with Operation Double Cross ASAP."

"Do we have enough evidence that the DPRK is behind that fire?" Gabler asked.

"It's enough for me," the president of the United States said without blinking an eye.

CHAPTER NINE

Prime Minister Lord Blancomb agreed with President Daniels's decision to implement Operation Double Cross, and the formal orders were transmitted to the commando units at The Farm. In the middle of the night, they boarded an MC-130E/H Combat Talon I/II—a C-130 modified to support US special operations--headed for Seoul [Seongnam] K-16 Air Base.

The team leader--American Daniel Kilgallon, previous service or rank unknown--met Sergeant First Class Park Min Joon, ROK [Republic of Korea] Black Beret Special Forces 707 Special Mission Group and his fourteen man operating teams (four females included) on the airport tarmac. 1st Sgt. Park was the designated co-second in command with SAS Master Sergeant Clive Lester. The American and British black-ops troops were allowed to sleep for six hours before moving surreptitiously into North Korea.

Now, all President Daniels could do was to wait and watch. She spent time in the Oval Office communicating with the two congressional leaders regarding their chosen problem areas—repair and maintenance of the infrastructure, and the general welfare of Americans.

With the shackles of internecine strife between the legislative and executive branches removed, Speaker Zimbrowski was able to move money and federal equipment all around the country to assist the volunteers in the reconstruction/repair projects, at least to get the process back in motion.

Majority Leader Nichols formed bipartisan and bicameral committees to move legislation and appointments along at a record rate. Thorny matters of taxation, appropriations, border security, health and welfare, racial contentions, prison reform, and foreign affairs—in conjunction with the White House—began to break with the traditions of unnecessary clumsiness and complexity that had plagued government since the inception of the republic. Sybil was gratified to see a good beginning of the new partnership with her, Zimbrowski, and Nichols.

It was 0200, EDT before the first news came in from the Double Cross operations unit in the field.

Team leader Kilgallon reported that the entire force and its equipment had crossed the DMZ and entered DPRK territory without incident; and, so far as they could tell, without being detected. Gen. Gabler thanked the lead members of the American, British, and Korean units for their efforts and courage.

The FBI investigation of the assassination attempt on the president reported its first inkling of progress at 0615 that morning. They were following a possible lead that suggested involvement by an OMG [Outlaw Motorcycle Gang] in weapons trafficking, which included military assault rifles and sniper rifles stolen from a West Virginia national guard armory. An FBI stakeout unit identified the man who was second in command of the East coast division of the Scimitars, described as a notorious ongoing criminal conspiracy and as a possible participant leadership role in the recent anti-American attacks which were put down by an unprecedented cooperation by US armed forces and law enforcement units. Trials were still underway for some of the most serious offenders, but prosecutors were hampered by lack of turncoat evidence.

The stakeout unit verified their man with photographs submitted for FBI facial recognition, then called for backup. The perpetrators were hard at work in a presumably vacant old warehouse loading wooden crates into semi-trucks for transport elsewhere.

The building was surrounded by dense forest, which was now teeming with combat equipped agents. Six agents with rappelling equipment were ready on the roof. They cut four holes in the roof big enough to allow passage of two men at a time using ultra high speed nearly silent saws. Two-man units stood ready at every first-floor level window, exit, and entrance.

"Mic check," SAC Dennis Clegg whispered.

He clicked his mike three times and received back two click responses from all teams.

Clegg whispered, "Enter on my 'zero'. Flash bangs and smoke bombs first. Gas masks in place. Guns on full auto. Be careful; try not to kill everybody. We need possible snitches."

Everyone took a deep breath and listened to the count, "Five... four... three... two... one... zero."

The old building lit up as if a hundred grenades had been tossed into its main floor at once. Smoke, bursts of blinding light, and the coordinated screams of the entering force paralyzed the criminals inside. A milli-second later, it was as if a host of giant locusts blasted their way into the building through every window door and holes in the roof.

the criminals—alleged criminals, to be legally correct—coughed, choked, fell to the floor, ran about aimlessly, and were subdued easily by the well-trained law enforcement intruders, hand cuffed with zip-ties, and rendered harmless in less than ten minutes.

SAC Clegg had his men set the now chastened "alleged" perps propped into sitting positions along the building's walls and began an intense, but quick interrogation.

The first question for each criminal was, "Where are the guns headed?"

Second was, "Who hired you; who's in charge?"

Third came a question related to the fact that none of the perps answered any question.

It was, "Who would rather turn state's evidence and gain immunity? and who wants to go to prison for most of the rest of their lives—no sex, no good food, no seeing family, no ball games. Might get out by the time you're seventy-five and decrepit?"

Five men whispered in the ears of their questioner and were swiftly segregated from the rest. The remainder were not particularly gently crammed into a prison bus still shackled and taken to the federal central holding center in Morgantown. The five were separated from each other. Each was given a large bottle of ice-cold water; their faces were wiped off with a clean moist cloth; and they were helped to folding chairs with comfortable cushions on the seats.

After learning all they could from frightened and finally cooperative men, the criminals were granted full immunity and entrance into the Wit-sec program in return for their testimony in court. None of the men knew very much about the operation; but, in aggregate, the special agents learned that the guns and ammunition had been stolen from three different armories with the help of complicit armed forces non-coms. They were to be transported to a list of fourteen different cities, presumably to start the insurrection all over again. No one could tell the agents much about a sniper, except that there was one Slavic-looking man with a purely evil looking face, who did not seem to belong and who spent most of his time cleaning and recleaning a beautiful long barreled rifle. One of the five reported that he had seen a ghillie suit in the gun's case.

One of the men appeared to be the ring-leader, maybe the leader of the entire transportation operation.

He told SAC Clegg that he thought the all-around jefe was a Scimitar leader named Jake "Big Man" Hennessy who might live in New Orleans. He received a ham and cheese sandwich as a reward. All five men were then taken away to federal holding in Chicago to keep them away from the hold-out perps.

The federal agents then spread out along the east coast to follow leads related to Big Man Hennessy. The bulk of the law enforcement energy was centered in New Orleans.

At noon, EDT, the Double Cross unit communicated again.

"Sorry we could not give you more frequent updates, but we had to be on strict radio silence. The countryside is crawling with hostiles," Kilgallon reported, his voice scratchy and fading in and out.

"No problem. Sit rep," Gen. Gabler ordered.

"Our Korean scouts are great. We are hiding in trees looking right at the Great Mansion. Everything seems to be copacetic so far—no WIA, KIA, and morale is good. Next check-in in about an hour."

President Daniels was in the Situation Room when Kilgallon called and nodded her pleasure for the good news thus far.

New Orleans PD, and the FBI linked up for a no-knock warrant service on a two story hundred-year-old house near the NASA Michoud Assembly Plant. According to NOPD and an online source, *Neighborhood Scout*, New Orleans itself as a whole is less safe than 95% of all the cities in the US; and Michoud village is the least safe neighborhood in the city. It is described as dangerous squared. Before Hurricane Katrina, Michoud had begun to suffer from disinvestment and urban decay. After Katrina, it was nearly as impoverished and ramshackle as the outskirts of the Dharav neighborhood in Mumbai, India.

The cops surrounded the house on J. Lafitte Avenue near the Malcolm Edwards projects after total darkness settled on the black polluted sky. All the windows were boarded up to protect against stray bullets. Watching through their night-vision, the agents could not detect anything moving, not even a stray dog. One sentry stood at the front door. The house was painted "haint blue" to frighten away ghosts. It made the house an only slightly different shade of grey to the naked eye or green through the NV goggles.

SAC NO Craig Jones sent SA Strickland, the blackest agent in the city, to deal with the sentry. He was able to do so without noise or even killing the man. The rest of the large force surrounded the building. NOPD officers cordoned off a six-block area to prevent escapes or injuries to citizens (criminal gangs excepted). It was Jones's decision to use stealth rather than upfront surprise or shock and awe. He sent teams of four agents to the front and rear entrances of the shotgun house. The doors were locked, but the locks were easily picked. Eight men were inside and in position around strategic points without disturbing any occupants.

Jones came in the second wave and had his men use infrared heat detecting devices to determine the presence or absence of occupants in the bedrooms. Only three bedrooms were occupied, one of which had small signatures indicating the presence of four children.

Two bedrooms had what appeared to be two adults in two separate beds, and the third room had two adults in one bed. SAC Jones ordered four men at each of the bedroom doors. The agents tried the doorknobs and found none of them to be locked.

He whispered, "On my count."

Every agent moved his or her lips as the SAC's fingers dropped—thumb… index finger… third finger.

Each team crept on rubber soled shoes into the blackness of the bedrooms undetected. One man stood at the bedside of each sleeper. Jones gave single click signal on his mic. The agents took off their NV goggles, put on face masks, and simultaneously dropped flash bang grenades.

The sleep befuddled and light dazzled occupants of the beds reacted with terror and bemusement. Despite their terrible reputations for violence, every adult was in cuffs and muffled before serious noise could erupt. The four children slept through the whole thing.

There were three more communications from the Double Cross team, the last at midnight.

"One hour to entry," Kilgallon said. "We'll all have our helmet cams on from then on."

NOPD police-women arrived at the Michoud house to gather up the four frightened children and took them to an emergency foster care shelter. The police and FBI agents put the adults in two armored vans and transported them to the Orleans Parish Federal Prison at 531 Broad Street. They were met halfway by three SWAT team vehicles for added protection. The convoy was trailed by two or three souped-up vehicles, but there were no incidents.

The convoy entered the prison facility through the rear entrance and escorted the prisoners to the holding cells in the basement. Each person—five men and one woman—was separated from the others and interrogated at about the same time.

SAC Jones matched the police department's mug shots against the faces of his prisoners and easily identified which man was Jake "Big Man" Hennessy. He entered Hennessy's holding cell with a stenographer and two guards.

"Well, Big Man, it's your day to shine—maybe your lucky day. We're gonna take a little walk to a comfortable interview room where you will have a chance to improve your situation."

"Fat chance," said the angry bushy faced man.

In the interview room, SAC Jones sat quietly and stared at Big Man until he began to fidget.

"Here's the thing, Hennessy. We have you dead to rights on illegal transportation of illegal firearms across state lines, for running an ongoing criminal enterprise, for three murders, and for conspiracy to mount an insurrection against the government of the United States of America. That gives you life in prison without parole at best. However, taken all together; and since the murders were premeditated and in furtherance of felonies; you are looking at the needle."

"Can't prove any of it."

"Oh, but we can. Your lady lied for you, but your four bosom buddies caved and are willing to testify for a consideration. However, you can escape the needle by coming clean about your other worse crime."

"What's that?"

"Criminal conspiracy and attempted murder of the president of the United States."

That came as a bolt out of the blue to the hardened criminal.

"Who says?"

"You know who, and you know that they know. Your goose is cooked unless you 'fess up right now to all of it. I will do everything I can to save your miserable life if you do, or I will be your worst nightmare if you don't."

"Lemme think on it."

"Here's a pencil and a piece of paper. You can write while I'm gone if you like. But I'm busy; so, you only get five minutes to make up your mind."

At 0100 sharp, Kilgallon communicated back with a terse, "We're in the palace. Get synced with our helmet cams. We're on our way to Kim Chin-Mae's quarters. Should be there in fifteen minutes or so if we don't get interrupted."

"Copy," said Gen. Gabler.

Actually, none of the other prisoners had been interrogated fully yet; and—while they were shaky—none of them had caved in enough to incriminate anyone— themselves or Hennessy. It was becoming something of a sticky-wicket for Jones. He waited ten full minutes then went back to Hennessy's interview room.

"Youse were out longer than five minutes, Fibby," Hennessy said.

"Got hung up. So, what's it gonna be, Big Man?"

"I'll take the deal, but you gotta swear you'll leave my girl and my family alone."

"Done. Start writing."

Jones was finally able to scare the other four men into confessions and agreements to testify. The woman—Hennessy's girlfriend—held out. Jones came to believe that she really did not know anything of significance and let her go.

Jones picked up Hennessy's yellow legal pad sheet with his confession and was frankly astounded that he copped to having plotted the presidential assassination and having hired the hit man, from among some survivalists who lived in the northern Michigan woods. The hit man was known by the Scimitar gang as George Smith, presumably a phony, but it was all that was available at the moment.

The director of the FBI ordered a extensive investigative operation to hunt down the name, and, if at all possible, the whereabouts of "George Smith".

"Call in every marker; pressure all the CIs in the three state areas; show George's photo in every city, Podunk town, farm, and under every bridge where the homeless sleep. Canvass every gun club, sporting goods store; and get together with every gun enthusiast up in those woods. Let's get results, Gentlemen."

It was impossible to be subtle or secretive about the FBI invasion. Every person in northern Michigan—young and old, whatever race, and any of the 52 genders—recognized a fibbie a mile away. They did not care for the federal government or its agents and were entirely disinclined to be communicative. The enterprise was a completely uphill walk.

The 0200 report from Kilgallon was terse but positive, "We have taken up positions at either end of the hallway from Cousin Kim's apartment. We have verification that there are only two people in the room, more accurately, only two heat signatures. If we're wrong, it's going to be a huge Charley-Foxtrot."

Gen. Gabler said, "Keep us on your video screen."

"Copy that."

CHAPTER TEN

Kim Myung Dac was a first cousin of the Dear Leader and Eternal General Secretary of the Party. That provided him a quick and important rise in the hierarchy of North Korea. He was not a stupid man. He recognized that it would not be healthy from him to appear to be overly ambitious, something of a genius, or a highly successful occupant of any position he was given. Mediocre was good; it was safe. Poor performance–so long as it was not public or embarrassing to his cousin–was something of a plus. So, lackluster Cousin Myung carefully sailed along under the radar and enjoyed his life as much as one could in the nerve-wracking higher echelons over which such a capricious leader presided.

He had grown obese, promiscuous, and lazy. As a result, he did not draw attention to himself as any kind of contender. This particular night, he had two pillow girls in his bed, a $4,000 large decanter of rare 23-year-old Pappy Van Winkle Kentucky Bourbon to share, and his choice of porno films passed down to him by his generous cousin. He had just smoked a joint and was settling into a pleasant state of lassitude thinking about how good his life was.

His bedroom door opened silently, and three men and two women walked in. They were dressed in black, and their weapons were matte black. Before he could recognize his plight, Myung's heart was penetrated by a direct hit from a silent crossbow. The two girls were too stoned to know or care about their surroundings, and they died from perfectly aimed arrows before they could feel pain or anxiety.

A week of walking the leather soles off their shoes was draining the strength and enthusiasm of the FBI special agents trudging along country roads in Northern Michigan, three miles outside Munising and within rock throwing distance of the Pictured Rocks National Lakeshore. The name derives from the irregular streaks of mineral stains on the face of the weathered-sculpted cliffs. The array of colors occured when groundwater seeped through the cracks and trickled down over the rock face. Iron solutes produce red and orange colors; copper, blue and green; manganese brown, grey, and black; limonite (a mixture of varied percentages of hydrated iron III oxide-hydroxide) which produces cream and white colors; and crystals of adamite which produce bright purple inclusions, are the most common color-producing minerals in the Pictured Rocks. The cliffs tower 50-100 feet up from the blue of Lake Superior.

Munising, population 2,300, is the county seat of Alger County and takes pride in its waterfalls, its basketball teams, and the sea caves of The Alger Underwater

Diving Preserve, a popular scuba-diving area in the Great Lakes. The Preserve offers clear water and diving attractions including intact shipwrecks, sea caves, and underwater interpretive trails. The manager of the preserve was a bluff, six-foot-tall, red bearded, man named Justin Greves. He was new to the area, and he was the object of the FBI agents' quest on that morning.

They piled the bed of their pickup with swim and scuba gear and drove to the parking lot of the preserve. Special Agent Trent Calloway walked to the office and booked a dive tour for the afternoon from Justin Greves for all six agents, who were posing as a university group. Young agents had been selected for this operation.

"You guys from down south?" Greves asked conversationally.

"Yeah, all Michigan State University-James Madison College Spartans."

"How are you goin' to do this year in Big Ten basketball?'

"Cheerful good losers as usual, we expect. You a Spartan?"

"Nope, I'm a ramblin' wreck."

"So, how're the Yellow Jackets lookin' for ranking in football in the ACC [Atlantic Coast Conference], Justin?"

"I don't follow that close, but I'm told that things are lookin' up for a change."

"Good luck."

As Trent and Justin chatted, the swim guide did not notice that the other five agents had gathered around encircling them.

"Ya'all got all your equipment, or do I need to fetch some rentals?"

"Actually, Justin. We have no intention of scuba diving."

Trent opened his cred-pak and showed his FBI credentials and badge. All the other agents had quietly pulled their credentials out; so, Justin could see them--and at the same time--see that he was surrounded and that resistance was futile.

Justin looked completely flummoxed.

"Ya'll say what?"

"You need to come with us to Lansing."

"For what. I think ya'll got the wrong fella."

"No, Sir. We have the goods, and you know it. Are you going to come along reasonably, or do we have to restrain you?"

"Am I under arrest?"

"Do we have to?"

"I guess not, I'll come just to find out what's goin' on." He was docile and fully cooperative.

"I need to change outta my dive stuff, okay?"

"Sure. We'll escort you."

Justin turned back towards the dive shack and began to walk slowly, talking a blue streak all the while.

Suddenly--just before they reached the front door of the dive shack--Justin bolted and sprinted towards the lake's edge. He paused to tense for a deep dive when Trent and Special Agent Tom Murphy tackled him and hand-cuffed his wrists behind his back. For good measure, they placed leg shackles and connected ankle and wrist shack-les to a heavy chain around Justin's waist. Two agents half dragged and half wedgie-walked the squirming Justin tippy-toe in a two man Mervin, pulling the reluctant red head up and forward by his tighty-whiteys and dropped him unceremoniously in the back of the SUV that had just pulled up. They headed to Lansing for a thorough interrogation in the basement of Lansing 54 A District Courthouse, lights and sirens clearing their way.

Sybil did not reply to the first three calls from the Swiss Legation handling US/DPRK diplomacy. A direct call came to the White House switchboard from North Korea, and Sybil refused to answer that one as well. The president of the Swiss Confederation called the Oval Office number directly, and Sybil answered that call.

"How nice to hear from you, Simonetta…President Maurer. To what do I owe the honor?" As if she did not know.

"Let's keep it informal between us girls, Sybil. I am trying to get the heat between the US and the DPRK to simmer down. I am speaking on behalf of the seven member/ministers of the *Bundesrat* [Swiss Federal Executive] to get you to communicate at least once with the Party Center, Chairman Kim. He is about to blow a fuse as you Americans like to say. He is accusing you…personally, of murder. Without casting aspersions, I fear that—in his present state of mind—he might just shoot off a nuke and start a conflagration around the world."

"Simonetta, whatever he is blathering about is nonsense," she lied, "I will be happy to transmit an official US government letter to the man, but it has to go through the Swiss Legation on Swiss Confederation letterhead paper; so, everything remains tidy. If it would suit you, I can dictate a letter to your stenographer who can type it under your letterhead. To move things along, I can have my chief of staff forward you a facsimile of my signature you can use and then destroy."

"All right. I agree to that arrangement. It is probably best for you and The Superior Person to keep things very much at arms-length. Please hold while I summon my *Stenograph*."

Four minutes later, Hilda Packer came on the line, "You may proceed whenever you wish," she said.

Sybil collected her thoughts for a moment then spoke slowly in formal, well enunciated English.

"Esteemed, Wise, and Respected, Leader Kim:

"It has come to my attention that a member of your personal and official family has died, perhaps by foul play. Sources from your foreign services have suggested that the United States of America might be implicated. I assure you that nothing could be farther from the truth. In fact, I do not believe anyone in our country could possibly penetrate your home and palace, one of the most secure places in the world. To think we could do such a thing would be to suggest that it is possible for us to bypass or subdue your security personnel and equipment. I am sure you would find that as outlandish as I do, Great Leader.

"Please consider my offer to assist you in your investigation of any crime that might have occurred and help in anyway you ask to help in the apprehension of the criminal. I hesitate to suggest, *Silchŏngahyŏngŭi Ŭiin* [Great Man, Who is a Man of Deeds], but it seems more than possible that the only person who could move with enough freedom within your most secure domain would have to be someone close to you. We have a saying in the West: 'an enemy will stab you in the chest; a friend will stab you in the back.' Perhaps you might give that thought some heed, Unique Leader.

"My government and I believe it is time for you to turn the direction of your guns inward instead of outward toward the sea. I am sure you will find the truth by so doing."

Your admiring friend,
Signed, Sybil Norcroft Daniels,
President of the United States

Frau Packer read the message back to the president. It was word for word perfect.

"Thank you, Madam President. Please do not take offense, but is it possible that you laid in on a bit thick?"

"Whatever do you mean, Hilda?" and she raised her famous one eyebrow of Question.

During the time President Daniels was negotiating her reply to Kim via the Swiss Legation, the FBI Special Agents were making some headway in the interrogation of Justin Greves. It took three hours to learn that Justin was a fake name, which came as no real surprise. They also learned that his real name was Thomas J. Jackson Rutherford, but he finally admitted that all his friends called him "Stonewall". The only other thing they learned by speaking directly to Stonewall was that he was born and reared in Jacksonville, Mississippi.

The FBI is nothing if not resourceful, and because this involved an assassination attempt on the sitting president, they applied their considerable resources to find out everything known about the man—his grades and high schools, girlfriends, a short dishonorable stint in the army, his lengthy rap sheet, and that he did a nickel in the Mississippi State Penitentiary in Jacksonville for armed robbery and aggravated assault. He was never found to merit parole; so, he completed his entire sentence.

The interrogators believed that they had reached a dead end and were frustrated. FBI Director Horace Eyring decided to intrude.

He called Trent Calloway and asked, "Is this Rutherford a man of great principle? of strong altruism? a tough never yielding hero?"

"Well, Director, I don't know which one of those he might be, but he won't budge. He won't listen to offers of bribery, and he doesn't seem to subscribe to any particular ideology. It appears that he is hard-wired not to snitch, and that's that. He even asked if we were going to torture him. He did not seem to be the least bit afraid of it. We tried everything we could think of, but we admit defeat. For the record, I am opposed to torture in any form; and, besides, I am sure it will not work in this case."

"All right, I want to send you our lead interrogator. This agent has succeeded in many difficult cases where everyone else failed. The agent will be in Lansing tomorrow morning."

SA Anne Barrows Kirkland walked into the Lansing District Courthouse and made a beeline for the basement interrogation room. She carried a large solid black leather messenger bag over her shoulder which appeared to be quite full.

"Hello, Gentlemen," she said quietly in a soft clear voice. "I have come to help. Don't think of me usurping your prerogatives. I will just be doing my job. I have been doing it for twenty-two years, and I like to think that I have learned some useful things. I will need a pretty free hand with the perp for a while. I need you not to try and interfere with what I'm doing, even with questions in front of the interviewee… what's his name?"

"Justin Greves is what he'll tell you, but his real name is Thomas J. Jackson Rutherford. He loves to tell us that his friends call him 'Stonewall'," Trent said and laughed briefly.

"Take me to my quarry, please, Gentlemen. I want to get started early."

SA Kirkland stepped into the interview room and stood facing Rutherford who was seated in an uncomfortable government issue steel chair which was bolted to the floor. He was shackled, and a big Swedish guard stood stolidly behind him.

"Hello, Stonewall. I am Special Agent Kirkland. I am going to ask you a few simple questions; so, we can get to know each other. Then, you can call me Anne, all right?"

Stonewall nodded his head.

"All right then. Stonewall, do you like to live?"

He looked at her quizzically but decided to play along with her silly questions.

"Yeah."

"What do you like best about being alive?"

"Huh?"

"Let's break it down, what's your favorite food."

"T-Bone."

"Your two favorite colors?"

"Hmmh, I guess green and blue."

"I knew that. Those are the colors of freedom. You like movies, Thomas?"

He was going to make a remark, but she asked a question before he could.

"What's your favorite drink?"

"Coors."

"Favorite dessert?"

"Vanilla ice cream with chocolate sauce."

"You're going to prison for a while, Stonewall. What are the chances you'll get to enjoy any of those things inside?"

"Probably between slim and none."

"I think you're right. Do you like to make love with women?"

"What a dumb question? Whatta you think I am?"

"Couple of more questions and I will be able to answer that. Do you like to make love to men?"

"Whaa-at!?" Stonewall shouted. "What gives...Do you think I'm a queer boy, Lady?"

"Let's find out. Answer my question, yes or no."

"NO!" he yelled in case anyone was getting wrong ideas about him.

"Let's see, what if you were jumped in the back of the laundry room one night, and the three big guys hold a shiv to your throat and tell you that you can submit without a fight, or they'll let you go and spread it all around the yard that you are an FBI snitch. What's your choice?"

"I don't think anybody's gonna think I'm queer enough to do that stuff."

"Really, it doesn't matter what your preferences are or what makes you sick. The situation I am asking you about happens dozens of times every day in our prisons. The warden and the guards give a blind eye to it. They tell me it helps guys let off steam, makes the prisons generally safer,"

"Safer for who?"

"Some other guys, I guess. Because once you become the big guy's girlfriend, you're stuck in the job for as long as the two of you are inmates. Did the agents tell you how long you can expect to be in?"

"Yeah… probably for life if they don't execute me."

"Think about that. Unless you're into that sort of thing, prison will be a long, long time; that's what they call 'hard time'."

"So what. I guess I'll just have to not think about it. I mean, what else can I do?"

"Maybe it's not so much what you can do, but more what I can do?

"Really, it's not much. But I can make some important changes with system to make it a little easier on you. I'll give it to you straight. You are going to be a lifer, but I have a say about where that is. You are young, good looking, and a hunk. The bruisers will be after you, but I can get you into the seg unit and protected from the monsters. I can even influence the kind of food you get. You were in the army for a while: did you like that stuff served on a shingle?"

"Hated it."

"I can get you better fare."

"How come? You the warden's girlfriend, Lady?"

"Not hardly, I can get you privileges because I get something important in return. You know what quid pro quo is?"

"Not really."

"Give a little to get a little."

"Whadda *you* get?"

"A yellow star on my forehead," she said with a smile… "No, really, I get good marks for getting you to give me information. I control the perks, and I can take them away in half an hour; so, you can't lie to me or to refuse to help me. I milk you for years, and the better you supply me, the better I treat you. I can have a soft heart… or… not. I am going to sit here for five more minutes without saying a word. Then, I am going to ask you a simple question: are you my CI, and am I your fairy godmother?"

CHAPTER ELEVEN

Everyone in the DOD and at the White House who was aware of the situation in Korea was on tenterhooks. There was rampant speculation about what the wonderful Juche⊠i Challanhan Thaeyang [Bright Sun of *Juche*]—as some scoffers mockingly used one of Kim's many titles, or just "the Dwarf" behind closed doors—would do next. The question was never far from Sybil's mind. Four days after her fateful telephone talk with "The Brilliant Leader" as his awe-struck sycophants were calling him these days, a small break through took place.

Sybil's secretary received a message from the Swiss Legation that Kim Yong-nam, the head of state for foreign affairs for the DPRK, wished to speak to her. She referred the matter to Secretary of State Fiona Del Giordia. The interchange of information took several days; but finally, Chairman Kim stated flatly that he would only speak to his equal. Very reluctantly, President Daniels agreed that she would once again have a telephone conversation with the capricious and irascible North Korean Despot and extortionist.

The wheels of justice moved swiftly in the case of Thomas J. "Stonewall" Jackson Rutherford, aka Justin Greves. After his interrogation by SA Anne Barrows Kirkland, he was transferred to the incarceration center at The Farm to await his final court appearances and assignment to a permanent federal prison—which would be determined by his usefulness or lack thereof. He had his bad days; but usually, he continued to be a veritable fountain of information. His memory was somewhat sketchy when it came to the name of the ultimate criminal leader who had been part of a loosely structured ring of eleven criminal chiefs who organized and supervised the recent attempted insurrection. All of them had escaped capture and left their underlings to bear the brunt of law enforcement and justice system displeasure.

Rutherford was actually happy to be in the extreme security of The Farm even if he was not completely enthralled by the accommodations. Even the mention of going to one of the federal "country club prisons" scared him straight, and he again found his voice. His foggy recollections cleared enough to give one name: Carmichael Alfonse Richards III who used to live in the Bronx; but, since he had come up in the world of crime, he now lived in a palatial mansion in Holmby Hills, a ritzy neighborhood in Westwood Los Angeles, near Beverly Hills. He had taken on a veneer of respectability as an importer/exporter of fine antique carpets and vases.

SAC FBI Los Angeles, Cliff Carter Canfield—known by his friends and enemies alike as "Triple C" was brought up to date and assumed control of obtaining a no-knock warrant and of organizing a strike force. Stonewall had informed SA Kirkland that the man was as a guy everybody was afraid of, even hitmen and human traffickers. So, Canfield organized what amounted to a small law-enforcement army and devised a top-secret plan for the apprehension of the man who was a twin perpetrator in his mind: the organizer of the insurrection against the United States, and the principle conspirator in the assassination attempt on the president. Triple C was no dummy: he realized that this assignment could either propel him into the inner circle of the DFBI or find him exiled to the west desert as a one-man FBI office.

Sybil's first appointment of the day was with Speaker of the House Shirley Zimbowski. Most of their conversations had been on facetime up to this date, but Zimbowski was very eager to share with the president what she and her national reconstruction and infrastructure repair blue ribbon committee had accomplished in such a short time.

"I got rid of every impedimenting law or policy that interfered with when and where construction and repair can take place, whether east or west of the Mississippi. The money you got from Treasury is now at work providing jobs and getting things built in record time. We found out that private companies could move through the regular issues of purchasing, surveying, clearing ground, demolition, and construction far more effectively than us feds can, at reduced cost, and on time.

I have sixty-two projects to show you that are nearing finish. You will be thrilled, Madam President. I have to admit that my hat's off to you for getting us all cooperating. Twenty-six dams will be safe by the end of the year and three thousand by the end of next year. We have major crews tearing apart the antiquarian piping systems in New York City, Chicago, Detroit, and St. Louis. I can't really predict when those projects will be completed.

She showed the president photographs of rising buildings, new pipes and utility lines being swapped out for the old and decaying systems, repaired highways, and completely replaced old railways.

Sybil said, "Shirley, I'm thrilled. Great work. I get reports in from all sorts of volunteers; it seems to me that the idea of making a new and better America has become a catch phrase of reality instead of just a political slogan."

Speaker of the House Zimbowski almost skipped as she left the Oval Office buoyed up for another day of honest work, something rather novel in her experience. She was also aware that the president was giving her the credit instead of the other way around which was even more novel.

Prime Minister David Lord Blancomb called at 1100.

"Madam President, I have a bit of news you may find interesting and even perhaps useful one day given the instability of the times in North Korea, Iran, China, and Russia."

"Glad to get any crumb I can," Sybil responded.

"This is top-secret, but our Atomic Energy Commission has done an inventory of our atomic capabilities and found that we have considerably more weapons grade plutonium than we thought we had, and it is due to our fine populist Wood-Jackson. He secreted away enough plutonium that we now have the biggest stockpile of civil plutonium in the world, mostly stored in the Sellafield nuclear plant in Cumbria. What was once a valued asset, is now viewed as a costly liability and a target for terrorists. Estimates suggest that our taxpayers currently spend £80m a year to store it safely and to stop it from falling into the wrong hands."

"I'm holding my breath, David. How much do you have?"

"110 tons."

"The cost is a serious drain on your already hurting economy, and the security risks are huge. The CIA reports that several North Korean and Iranian agents have been seen poking around in the Cumbria area and around the Sellafield plant over the past year. I would say that you have a problem on your hands, My Friend."

"Indeed, Sybil. But I did not call to whine or complain. Rather, I would like to offer you a win-win deal for you and us."

"I'm listening with perked-up ears."

"What if we sold you half and going prices, and you rebuild your stockpiles unbeknownst to the Great Leader and his minions? Our intelligence services are supplying us with information almost daily about threats against you and efforts to undermine your economy. Sadly to say, but the time may come, and not long from now, that you will need our fissionable material."

"Besides the decent business deal, what do you get out of this?"

"I was waiting for you to ask. You gain by not having to put out any payment per se. We gain by having the plutonium deal result in payment in full for our dreadful reparations costs."

Sybil N. Daniels was used to processing quickly and making serious decisions rapidly, "You have a deal, Mr. Prime Minister. I'll have my people get with your people, as they say in Hollywood. Say hi to Millie and the children for me."

"And my regards to Charles, and to Drake, Cerisse, and the children from Millie and me."

Sybil ruminated throughout the day about whether or not to have the requested communication with Kim Jong Un. As near as she could tell, he had not demonstrated any decrease in his belligerence. That changed with a sat phone call from the carrier *Theodore Roosevelt* on watch in Korea Bay.

"Good day, Madam President," came the scratchy somewhat delayed voice of Admiral Trescott, the commanding officer of the carrier.

"Good day, Sir. What is your sitrep?"

"Something moving. We have been watching the harbor line all morning. With no communication to us, the shore guns have pivoted so that they are all directed towards the north. We plotted the potential trajectories, and every cannon would hit North Korean territory if fired. Our reconnaissance planes encountered no hostiles when they flew over the lines of artillery aimed at Seoul. As of noon today, every big gun has either been moved out of the area or its muzzle is pointed in the opposite direction."

"What is your take on that, Admiral?"

"Little Man blinked first."

Sybil said, "All right, Admiral, let's back off a bit more. Take the carrier groups to the middle of the international waters and tread water there. I will let you know what happens at my end; but for now, let's not count our chickens before the eggs are laid."

"Aye, aye, Ma'am."

Sybil contacted Ferdinand Delasse at the Swiss Legation and asked him to arrange for Simonetta Maurer, president of the Swiss Confederation, to join Ferdinand and Sybil in a conference call with the DPRK officials.

Sybil told President Maurer that, "I have a plan that makes it seem worth the dictator's and the country's effort to save itself and to assist them to have a place among the family of nations. Even the Soviet Union and the PRC did that."

She explained her idea and got a fairly insipid but grudgingly positive agreement to explain the Swiss point of view.

Again, the call tracked its stubborn way from the Oval Office to the Swiss Legation Office to Kim Han Jin in the DPRK Taedonggang River Swiss office to Kim Yong-nam, the head of state for foreign affairs for the DPRK whose office was located in the same building in the *Ryongsong* Residence [Residence No. 55] as the *Ryŏngdojaka Katchuŏya Hal Phungmorŭl Wanbyŏkhake Jinin Chikaehanŭn Jidoja* [Dear Leader, Who is a Perfect Incarnation of the Appearance that a Leader Should Have].

Mr. Kim reported to his callers that the *Choekosaryŏnggwan* [Commander-in-Chief] was at present, indisposed; but he would be on the line shortly.

"Shortly" was just under an hour, but finally the Great One's voice sounded over the scratchy static on the line. He was using a filter to deepen his voice because one of his aides had told him that his great masculinity would be more manifest if he did.

"Hello, to my friend, the Swiss president. We in the People's Democracy appreciate what you and your fine neutral nation have done to further peace in our region. I acknowledge the presence of Mrs. Daniels on the line as well."

It was a clumsy calculated insult, but Sybil considered the source and ignored it.

President Maurer said, "Greetings to you Great Leader. I am only a facilitator here..."

There was a pause for translation and explanation.

"... and I will turn the conversation over to you and President Daniels. At her request, I will remain on the line to listen. We will record this historical moment, if you agree."

It was another one of those chances to be seen as a leader on the international stage equal to the presidents of the United States and Switzerland.

"Of course, of course. We have nothing to hide."

President Daniels began to speak and got right to the point, "Great Leader and *Kongsanjuŭi Miraeŭi Thaeyang* [Sun of the Communist Future], I bring you the greetings of the American and the Swiss people; and I also bring to you for your consideration a proposal already agreed upon by President Maurer and me."

"Can we be ready to hear an honest and respectful proposal?!" Kim asked with scornful sarcasm.

"Yes, that is exactly what we have to offer, Chairman," President Maurer said, to back up President Daniels.

"This our proposal for your consideration, Chairman." said Sybil, "We suggest that you and your country gradually demilitarize to a level of a defensive military force similar to that maintained by Switzerland. We know you have offensive nuclear capabilities. You can adopt that demilitarization stance and permit international monitoring with free access by the appropriate monitoring body, and you will trade away those offensive weapons in return for a UN designation declaring the DPRK to be a neutral country. We have done our diplomatic homework and have obtained conditional agreement for the designation and the protection of China, Russia, South Korea, and the United States. It will result in gradual reversal of sanctions, opening of trade avenues, and freedom to travel in safety.

"And you will never have access to both eastern and western financial institutions. North Korea will be heralded from within and without to be a winning end state. With such a pivot, you will become the leader of the Switzerland of the East, and your nation will take its place in the United Nations, and trade organizations of East and Southeast Asia. It will cost you no money. Actually, you will save huge amounts of money by reducing the cost of being secure as far into the future as we can predict."

CHAPTER TWELVE

President Daniels hoped against hope that she was making the right decisions: giving the United Nations her blessing for North Korea to become part of the mainstream multination body with all of its attendant prestige; ordering the US fleet out of the *Choson Namhe* [South Sea of Korea}, the East Sea [Sea of Japan], and the West Sea [Yellow Sea]. She further guaranteed the DPRK that the US navy would cease and desist from traveling within the Japanese archipelago, near Sakhalin, Russia, and the Korean Peninsula, and would confine its voyages to the Pacific Ocean and avoid the several nearby seas.

Finally—after verification that all DPRK nuclear apparatuses, fissionable materials, missiles, and commerce with individuals, companies, and countries which have a history of trading in the materiel that could be used to produce missiles loaded with thermonuclear weapons had been removed from the Democratic Republic's land and commerce, recognition would be granted. At least Kim Jong Un had agreed to Sybil's deal; that was a pretty good start. It was now just a matter of waiting and hoping.

It was not a matter of her enjoying her sofa to do knitting or quilting while her pleasant husband enjoyed chess with the children. She did have a fairly major, and rather long neglected project. She had to get elected—technically not "re-elected". Her Republican and Democrat opponents had been attending to their duties during the usual eighteen to twenty-four-month election–or silly season–to get themselves elected in her place. It must have seemed like the dream situation for them because the incumbent was not campaigning; her popularity was at an historic nadir; and everything she did or attempted to do was of such a serious nature that she just kept on accumulating enemies. Two months ago, no one in the country—well, one person—believed that Sybil Norcroft Daniels would have a chance.

Then came the assassination attempt, and Sybil acquitted herself as a calm and courageous president. People began to remember the time of the insurrection differently; Sybil was the veritable poster girl defender against bullies and the cold fierce leader of a suffering nation against its enemies within and without now. They remembered further back to the time when England--of all countries—attacked our ships and our homeland. She handled that adroitly.

England came to our help once again, and together we put North Korea in its place and found a way for it to end hostility and to become a member—if not fully friendly—nation among nations. The severe economic downturn due to the insurgency had been met head on by the plucky woman; and she won, even though the country was not all the way back. By dint of her indominable personality, she was getting one of the jobs done that all Americans believed in—reconstruction and repair of the infrastructure. There was more to be done, but Americans were back to having jobs and doing what had to be done. America was becoming its great self again.

Her popularity and favorability rating began to grow, then climbed steadily, then frankly soared. Her new friends--the Speaker and the Majority Leader with their companies of followers–began to lend their endorsements and support, which helped very considerably. There were one and a half months before election day, and all the pundits agreed that she had more than an even chance to win the election by better than a nearly even margin. That is, if Sybil and the country could be spared another calamity.

Acting on the information given him by his new CI Thomas J. "Stonewall" Jackson Rutherford, SAC FBI Los Angeles, Cliff Carter Canfield—"Triple C"—moved his force of FBI agents from Los Angeles to work from the Beverly Hills PD building to prepare a workable plan to arrest Carmichael Alfonse Richards III Alphonse Richards III who now lived in a palatial mansion in Holmby Hills. Because of her excellent work in finding out the name of the possible mastermind of the attempted assassination of the president, Triple C requested the services of SA Anne Barrows Kirkland. Besides, it looked good to have females and minorities on his squad to show his leadership qualities.

The police chiefs of Los Angeles and Beverly Hills offered their SWAT teams and metropolitan police forces to aid in the capture of the powerful crime lord, and an all-day planning session among the police and the FBI agents took on what amounted to planning of a military operation. Service of the no-knock warrant was scheduled for two A.M. the following night, and the level of secrecy was on the order of the preparations for D-Day. Beginning at midnight, the small army moved quietly into every entrance of Beverly Hills, Bel Aire, and Holmby Hills. When the law enforcement officers were ensconced in an empty property surrounded by high walls, metropolitan police officers blocked every entrance and exit. They then visited every home on every street for three blocks around the suspect house and ordered the occupants—most of whom were none too happy about it—to evacuate to a tent shelter hurriedly set up for the purpose.

Intelligence officers assured the strike team that Richards was at home and presumably in his bed. At 0130 the armada of SWAT vehicles, police cars, and ambulances slowly drew to within half a block from their destination—1245 Charing Cross Road, half a mile from the historical monument, Playboy Mansion. Other than the police presence, the streets were empty and silent. At 0145, SWAT teams were in place by every entrance to the large residence, and helicopters had lowered two teams to the elegant house. A cordon of police vehicles surrounded the property so tightly that a stray cat would not have been able to get through.

At 0200, every unit moved forward. Skilled lock-smiths quietly opened each door and silent teams of combat experienced officers and agents slipped inside the mansion. Each man and woman had a blueprint of the place on his or her iPhone; and, according to their plan, they dispersed throughout the house to cover every bedroom and the security office. The inside of the house was pitch black, but that was not an issue for the entering force since they had night vision goggles. Their level of stealth was so complete, that they encountered no guards.

Three former military black-ops noncoms found four sleeping guards in a comfortable theater room and subdued them swiftly and silently. A roving guard walked along the hallway where Carmichael Alfonse Richards III and his current paramour, an exotic dancer named Candy Striper—presumably a stage name—were known to be sleeping.

Triple C tapped his mic twice, the signal for entry. Five of the most experienced FBI rapid response agents—since it was technically a federal operation—slipped into the huge bedroom on a two-inch thick carpet and stood by either side of the California long king-size bed. Carmichael was snoring, splayed on in his boxer shorts, and Candy was curled up in the sleek black silk sheets. She was wearing a sheer flesh colored silk nighty. An agent put a hand over each sleeper's mouth and announced loudly:

"Federal agents. Warrant! You are under arrest for attempted murder. Get up slowly; place your hands behind your heads, fingers interlocked."

The crime lord and his floozy complied with alacrity. The lights in the room were now blazing, and couple had not had time to adjust their pupils to the new sun level brightness. They were half asleep and moved like robots.

"Kneel down. Now lie on the floor on your belly, spread out your arms, wrists down."

They were handcuffed and escorted from their bedroom--dressed as they were--to waiting jail buses and handcuffed to the bus floors along with their ten chagrined security guards. They drove under heavy security guard—including motorcycle cops–to the Civic Center district of Los Angeles. Uniformed officers lined Temple Street while the convoy holding the probable attempted assassinators of the president approached the courthouse. The security increased as they neared 255 East Temple Street. They entered the rear of the Edward R. Roybal Federal Building and United States First Street Courthouse. Each perp received two guards who escorted them to the holding cells, a rather forbidding area of Los Angeles. The twenty-one story red stone tower and side buildings stand next to the Metropolitan Detention Center and behind the Federal Building and Post Office.

Each man and the one woman was assigned a public defender before the assistant district attorneys spoke a word to any of them. The perps were handcuffed to steel bars stretching across the top of the narrow table between them and the inquisitors. To make absolutely clear the security risk the perps were considered to be and the disdain in which they were held by the cops and jailers, their feet were bare, and their ankles were shackled to floor screw rings.

With some difficulty and no particular effort on the part of their public defenders, the name and address of every detainee was obtained; and the long interrogation process began. Purposefully, the lower ranked people were questioned first—actually beginning two hours after they were placed in cells.

The time-honored tradition of letting the person to be interrogated sit nervously in shackles to make them nervous and to weaken their resolve was in full force. They were not given food or water until noon, and every water bottle used by the detainee was taken away to provide surfaces containing DNA. Food was a dry crust of unbuttered white goo bread. Small food, drink, or walking about in the interrogation room to stretch their legs, were gradually increased perquisites doled out as the several detainees came forth with tidbits of useful information. The weaker, lower echelon perps who cracked and supplied serious information were fed piping hot meals of coffee, porkchops, baked potatoes, mixed vegetables, and vanilla ice cream for dessert—all served on paper plates and cups and a flimsy blunt balsa wood spoon.

Care was taken to be sure that the hungry holdouts got to watch their once "die-for-each-other" pals become "dirty rats" and receive rewards for doing so. By midnight, the exhausted hold-outs all capitulated and received hamburger patties, French fries, and cold water. They were allowed to sleep.

Then, SA Anne Barrows Kirkland, looking refreshed, bright-eyed, and bushy tailed, skipped into the room and bestowed her cheery perfect dental creation smile and began the process that had worked so well during her career.

"Hi, Mr. Richards, I'm Anne, what do you prefer to be called?"

"Called away," Alphonse griped.

Anne laughed.

"I guess you're quite a corker. Your friends told me about your ability to make a good joke out of almost any situation. Is that right?"

"I guess so, if you say so."

"I have a few questions Alphonse, if that's okay with you."

He shrugged. It was as if he had been reading from the same script SA Kirkland was using.

For two unrelenting hours the agent and the perp—not yet officially a criminal—asked questions and fielded answers which went from comfortable, minor, and general, to personal, probing, and serious, and finally to hard, angry, and threatening. By that time, Carmichael Alfonse Richards III was weary and confused, and he had learned what an encyclopedia of information Agent Kirkland had come armed with to the interview room. By midnight, he knew the jig was up, and he was reduced to explaining why he did what he did, why he was chosen by the higher ups to run the insurrection and to organize and fund the assassination attempt. He also named names to obtain what minimal percs he could hope for. The only leniency he could wring out of the femanazi tormenting him was a promise of a life sentence without parole to be served in the Lancaster State Prison.

After a year-long investigation, Richards and Rutherford were tried together in Los Angeles for attempted assassination of the president, incitement of insurrection; multiple murders, tortures, robberies, extortions, drug kingpin charges, pandering for prostitution, arson, and for operating an ongoing criminal conspiracy. The trial was three weeks in length because of the time required to list and summarize the huge number of crimes and the associated evidence. The jury deliberation was something of a record for its brevity—sixty-seven minutes, which included time out for a soda and candy bar and to prepare the documents.

Guilty on all counts. Sentenced to forty life sentences without the possibility of parole. After secret in-chamber discussions with the FBI agents, Judge Karl Duprie imposed an addition to the sentence. Both men were ordered to serve their time in the maximum Federal Penitentiary in Terre Haute, Indiana. Nearly all federal prisoners sentenced to death are housed there, and Richards and Rutherford were housed and treated as if they had been sentenced to death. The difference for them was that theirs was a living death.

Both appealed to change the location of their incarceration based on their statement that the FBI agents had promised them "country-club" prisons. Their appeals for new trials or even hearings on their requests were denied.

When a friend and confident asked SA Anne Barrows Kirkland about her having made such promises, she said with a soda cracker expression, "I lied."

Sybil, Charles, their daughter and son-in-law, and their grandchildren sailed through the grueling but short election process. They went on the stump as infrequently as Sybil's campaign managers would allow; and, in a striking reversal of the animosity directed towards her during the worst crises she faced for the country, all of that was now looked at as heroic and fully laudable. Everywhere she gave a speech, she was accorded a level of enthusiasm usually reserved for populists by their adoring bases. By the time she was elected president in November--thereby justifying her presence in office—she had garnered the largest plurality in history and lost only twelve electoral college votes. Sybil felt as if she had aged ten years during the last two, but she could not keep a satisfied smile from her face, even if she had tried.

Drake Farrer, her son-in-law—ever the realist—remarked over family dinner once the inaugural hoopla died down, "Betcha a milk-shake that this peace and plenty and the happiness it brings does not last more than the first quarter of your new presidency."

CHAPTER THIRTEEN

Drake was wrong about some of the elements of his prediction, but he still won the ice-cream cone. Two weeks following Sybil's second swearing-in, a crisis hit. It was perhaps the worst yet in her presidency even though it did not begin with bloodshed. Abraham Lincoln had seen the problem coming over decades during his life, but secession came abruptly along with his ascension to the presidency. He was elected president November, 1860. Immediately thereafter, seven southern states seceded before his inauguration December 20, 1860. On April 12, 1861, the first hostilities of the American Civil War began at Fort Sumpter in Charleston Harbor. By June, eleven states had seceded.

In the modern era of President Sybil Norcroft Daniels, it only took two weeks for formal secession dec[1] larations—plural—to be filed with federal district courts in Fairbanks, Honolulu, Denver, Sacramento, Salem, Montpelier, Austin, Lansing, and San Juan, Puerto Rico. The presenters offered a patchwork of oddly shaped proposals for establishment of multiple new and sovereign countries and division or unions of states to alter the shapes of the country within the territory of the United States of America as it had stood on Sybil's inauguration day. Civil and legal hostilities started the same day, and Sybil was faced with the reality—absurd as it might have seemed on that joyous occasion—that she was facing Lincoln's problem: save the union at all costs.

Sybil had only heard very distant rumblings of the discontent that was brewing, and even then, she had no appreciation of how earnest the would-be secessionists were. Frankly, she had dismissed them all as the work of crackpots, but it was plainly evident that she could no longer do so. She discussed the problems of separatism, autonomism, and outright secessionism—all of which were being proposed to the courts—with the Speaker, the Senate Majority Leader, the Secretary of Homeland Security, and the Attorney General, in a secret meeting held in the cabinet room.

"Can't we just ignore them and let them go away on their own account?" she asked.

"I don't think so," Speaker Zimbrowski said. "I have been traveling all over the country dealing with this infrastructure repair business, and I have had a chance to talk to people in every corner of the nation. It would be an exaggeration to say that they are everywhere, but there are groups of serious minded and well-informed people spread out more than any of us here might have imagined. I think we had better take them seriously now or pay a heavy price not too far in the future."

HS Secretary Gwendolyn Armistad spoke next, "Madam President, I got my PhD in history. My dissertation was on the process of secession. I have taken a lifelong interest in the subject since it keeps coming back again and again. This time seems more serious, especially since the many disparate groups are beginning to discover that there is strength in numbers. Most of the recent filings have been by like-minded groups and most recently by two or three consortiums that are arguing the principles involved as well as their own particular desire for change."

"Madam Secretary, share some of that history with us."

"I thought you'd never ask. I wouldn't want my parents' hard-earned money that went towards my education to go to waste. I'll be brief, however. For twenty or thirty years, the politics of slavery and abolition had been changing and were beginning to escape the bounds of compromise. Both sides hardened, and it was clear when Lincoln, the Republican, and Douglas, the Democrat, ran for president in 1860 that there was a real possibility that the South would secede if Lincoln was elected. John C. Calhoun was a rabid defender of slavery and had near total support in the Democrat party and in the South. He swore never to compromise. Lincoln could see it coming and felt that it was inevitable the major changes would have to be made. Others on the opposite political and ideological poles thought that war was not only inevitable, but a good way to settle things once and for all.

"Lincoln hoped that his oratorical skills and his reasonable approach would carry the day, but the country began to fragment the day he was elected. My point, Madam President, is that we in government and the judiciary cannot hide from this. Like Lincoln, we need to do something now and not let it get beyond the point of no return."

"Isn't this a problem for the judiciary... all the way to the Supreme Court? Let them finish it? I mean, the Constitution is clear about this, is it not?"

The Attorney General answered her, "Madam President, this is not simply a legal disagreement. This is broader and deeper. It is my opinion that you may be able to defuse some of the explosiveness of this movement before the complainants come to believe that violence is their only option. It has to be worth a try, at least."

"Do all the rest of you agree?"

They all nodded yes, some considerably less enthusiastic than the rest.

"You know, I'd rather be poked in the eye with a sharp stick, but I will make time to see them all--and all at once--in the next day or two. Talk about a lose-lose thankless job," Sybil said.

The meeting in the cabinet room was composed of a group of diverse characters as unusual for the White House as the time when newly elected Andrew Jackson opened its doors to his old pals—a drunken, disheveled, misbehaving, mob. It took the Secret Service and the Chief Usher of the White House over an hour to get them to sit in chairs, not to put their boots on the beautiful polished conference table top, and to surrender their guns temporally amidst yelling about the Second Amendment. The presidential guard unit had serious misgivings about allowing President Daniels even to walk into the room.

The room had acquired a mixed scent of eau de manure, cigar smoke, neglected arm pits, and Old Spice cologne. Some of the men, lacking a spittoon were hawking up goobers onto the fine carpet.

"Welcome, Ladies and Gentlemen," the president said, knowing that she was stretching the definition a bit. "What you bring to my attention today has been cooking in the country since the Revolution. Apparently, you have something new to add—a potential union of secessionists with a petition to be heard seriously as a group and not just as separate separatists."

They got a laugh out of that which helped to break the ice.

"I also appreciate that you have democratically chosen a spokesperson who can bring some order to what is a remarkably complex issue. I assure you that I have done my homework, but I am going to turn the time over to Mrs. Adelaida Maria Landreneau from the great state of Louisiana, your chairperson."

Mrs. Landreneau was a regal presence dressed in her best French Creole finery: a brightly colored full skirt with a tight bodice, a cashmere shawl, fragile shoes, a well-trimmed large hat, and long white gloves. She carried a lacework handkerchief, an ornate fan, and an especially out of place parasol. She could easily have stepped out of an eighteenth-century parlor in New Orleans.

She proved herself not to be a caricature when she began to talk in her soft, educated Creole patois.

"Madam President, it is my pleasure and privilege to address you and to speak on behalf of my fellow secessionists. Let me summarize something of the secessionist movement as it is today. We can leave the arcane history to another day.

"I will give a thumbnail sketch of the several entities represented here today. But, first, let me tell you that each movement here has its own reasons to secede from the union or to change its character within the union. I'll start with some definitions—present here today are separatists who include both autonomists and secessionists. There are no theoretical contrasts here; all must be part of active movements with living, active members seeking greater autonomy and/or self-determination for a geographic region of the country. We do not represent anyone except citizens/peoples of a defined conflict area, and none of them come from other countries.

The different—but all acceptable—seekers of autonomy from the government include different sources for their discontent, different regions of the country, and may or may not be part of a platform of a political party. So, we have:

- *De facto* states: for regions seeking de facto autonomy from the United States government,
- Proposed states: leaders are here today to announce a proposed name for their seceding sovereign state.
- Proposed autonomous area: for movements toward greater autonomy for an area but not outright secession, such as for local governments to have legitimized *de facto* autonomous control over a region.

- Government-in-exile: for a government based *outside* of the region in question, but still American legally maintaining its attachment to the USA, with or without control exercised by the US government.
- For political parties involved in their own political system and for their own reasons to be allowed to push for autonomy or secession.
- Among us are militant organization, who seek to exercise their rights under the Second Amendment to form de facto legal and autonomous armed organizations and to be free of being designated as terrorist organizations.
- Advocacy groups: for non-belligerent, non-militant and non-politically designated entities.
- And finally, there are several ethnic/ethno-religious/racial/regional/and/or religio us group. Think of the Mormon movement to form the State of Deseret in the mid-eighteen hundreds as an example.

"The defining issue behind all modern-day secession is the unity of a *minority* geographical section defending a distinct set of institutions that are believed to be under attack. The original federal Union that shared the exercise of power with the states strengthened the concept of secession, and we intend to pursue that argument to its logical conclusion. We have history on our side; Thomas Jefferson was a very strong advocate of states rights, and that advocacy led to secession. There is no reason to doubt that it could happen again. While my fellow secessionists and I are dedicated to bringing about secession, most of us do not want separations to come about as the result of bloodshed. We are here to ask you to take notice, to help the process of separation be a safe and orderly one."

"Mrs. Landreneau, I have agreed to listen and learn. Under our constitution you have the right to speak your piece. However much I might strive for an open mind, I cannot neglect my oath. I am bound to protect the United States against all enemies, within and without the country," President Daniels said.

"We have more to say, more for you to digest before you make your decision, Madam President."

CHAPTER FOURTEEN

The cabinet room took on a different quality: a tinge of anger, a sense of impending conflict, and a professorial attitude rather than a dispassionate discussion among equals or at least with a willing pupil. Sybil listened intently, but it was becoming evident to her that she was in a roomful of opponents. Perhaps not yet enemies, but there was a change in the temperature in the room as if someone had turned down the thermostat.

Mrs. Landreneau was clearly aware of the change and wanted to bring the president back to her original attitude of a willing listener.

"Madam President, please hear us out before forming an action opinion about how to deal with the information we bring. I am telling you the truth, and whether or not you accept the conclusions posed by the reality, it is still a very real condition within the United States. I know that this has been more than a mouthful, but it will become clearer as I tell you about our several disparate organizations. It is good that you are recording my message, and we have prepared a written memo. We have:

- "A resurgence of the historical *Círculo Dorado* [Golden Circle] first advocated in the1850s by a group they called the Knights of the Golden Circle. It's avowed purpose was to expand the number of slave states, to have and to expand the number of slave states today is a frank part of their plan. The movement proposes that it remain under the umbrella of the United States, until it can accomplish its original vision—that of annexing Mexico [to be divided into 25 new slave states, Central America, northern South America, Cuba, and the rest of the Caribbean sovereignties, annexed into the United States at first, then, later to become a separate autonomous nation going its own way. The movement's leader refuses to give his name but insists on being known as 'a member of the order'."

- "Cascadia a bio-region which includes the present states of Washington, Oregon, Northern California, parts of Idaho and Montana, Southern Alaska, and include British Columbia and parts of Alberta, Canada. The bioregion is created within the watersheds of the Columbia and Fraser river valleys that flow through British Columbia, Washington and Oregon. It stretches from South East Alaska in the North, to Northern California in the South, and east as far as the Yellowstone Caldera. This fact gives the Cascadia bio-region its continental and tectonic boundaries.

"One of the most important arguments for this particular movement towards secession is that Cascadia will soon become one of the world's largest economies, generating nearly $1 trillion dollars in GDP. That is fact, not fancy. Its primary industries will be farming and technology. The government would—of necessity--be left-leaning, probably democratic socialist with a focus on environmentalism to save it from the descent into destruction of the planet going on in the US and most of the rest of the world.

"The Pacific Northwest already fully embraces Cascadia and identifies with the region vigorously. Cascadian flags fly over major sporting events. They have a flag—the Cascadia Doug Flag which includes a large Douglas Fir tree. The Cascadia endeavor is a grassroots social movement whose purpose is to empowering individuals and communities throughout the Pacific Northwest. It is and will be centered on the things that define its unique regional character. Its proponents seek to increase the independence of the Cascadia bioregion – socially, politically, economically and environmentally.

"The Cascadia Movement seeks fundamental change, the US is too large and therefore too ponderous to change. There are fifteen to twenty social justice movements, like Black Lives Matter, environmentalism, divestment from fossil fuels, and divestment of private prison complexes to name a few examples. People want change, and that is exactly what the Cascadia Movement is about. We have to leave the United States and Canada to accomplish that. It is a social movement, not a political one. Politics are part of it for some, but we are much more interested in getting people active in their communities right now, building towards a positive vision, as well as creating an inclusive movement for real impact throughout the Pacific Northwest. Up to now, we have not undertaken any political organizing or lobbying; but our time has come."

- "The State of Jefferson movement has been around for a long time, Madam President. As far back as 1941, the idea of forming a new U.S. state including southern Oregon and northern California was put forward. The pertinent counties were in agreement, and the movement would probably have succeeded but for one small thing: bombs were dropped on Pearl Harbor. The idea, however, lives on. It is touted as a completely logical addition of a 51st state. The argument by the north is that one-third of California is undergoing taxation without representation. Remember that argument? Well it is as pertinent now as it was in 1776. Declarations must be filed under Article One, Section Three of the California Constitution for a redress of grievances due to lack of representation, and our declarations from the counties are well underway.

"There is a difference: Oregon is not presently involved. It could join up later once the new state is created. Understand, that each state has to follow its own state Constitution in order to secede. 51% of California lives below the northern boundary of Los Angeles. That gives Southern California a very improper voting advantage. The area of the State of Jefferson has to pay taxes for all those careless fires, air pollution from too many vehicles, and on and on. Southern California has 114 representatives to our mere 6. It is not fair or just, and we want out. We don't want to have to pay an equal share of California's two trillion-dollar debt. We shouldn't even owe the 1/3rd based on land mass, since we have not incurred the costs. Let them run their own cockamamie liberal state, and we will run our own fiscally sound one.

"We have only half of the fuel we need for an agricultural state. We can grow the food; they can produce the fuel; and we can share on a fair basis. We want a constitutional republic, like we asked for in the Declaration of Independence. We want a minimalist government that lets us keep our liberty. We can take care of ourselves. We can do without all those failed social and regulatory schemes, and the tax burdens the people endure for those wild give-away schemes. We can't afford the present California bureaucracy. The arrangements are nutty: the part time legislators work for only sixty days. The current state has 570 state agencies; we don't want things done that way. For example, as soon as the State of Jefferson comes into being, we will eliminate unnecessary bureaus like the state roads department and give the federal funds to our counties; so, they can make their own jobs as they want and need. We also don't need a state police force. Our county cops can do better for a third of the money. The money California wastes in a month would fund us for a year. We are sick of it and want a change now."

- "Coloradoans seek to divide, and petitions are meeting with considerable enthusiasm. The division is rural v. urban and conservative v. liberal. It is more likely than not that they will end up in federal courts."
- "The Kingdom of Hawaii: There has been an active Hawaiian Sovereignty Movement for many years which regularly hosts constitutional conventions to

return to the historical monarchy which existed until the islands were annexed by the United States. They really have only one goal which is to restore original Hawaiian traditions and provide free health care for all and a number of other quite generous social democratic benefits. The proposed kingdom plans to include all the eight major islands and all territory within the state. Its economy would be based on tourism and agriculture. The people proposing the Kingdom point out that the State of Hawaii generates around $70 billion in GDP. They have full confidence that they can function in perpetuity with the monarchy—a parliamentary monarchy—restored. The proposed flag is the Hawaiian flag waved upside down, symbolic of the movement."

- "The Second Vermont Republic Movement harbors a desire for independence from the days of the Revolution to form a nation independent of America and Britain. This time around Vermont has--for the past decade—been developing a movement to declare independence as the Vermont Republic. The movement has gained legs and can not easily be ignored. Vermont would remain a largely an agrarian society generating $25 billion dollars of GDP. The plans are to bring about a social democratic government similar to Austria, Finland, Sweden, and Switzerland—all of which have been quite successful."

- "The New England Independence Movement has at least 6,000 adherents, but the movement does not do polls, nor does it publish its numbers. The movement is based upon recent history which has led to the belief that the US federal government has become too divisive, and based on partisan politics, more recently on populism. The leaders of the movement and its followers take a non-partisan stance on US politics, but instead work to focus locally to unite New Englanders in a quest to regain the fundamental promise of the founding fathers of the United States: Life, Liberty, and the Pursuit of happiness for all.

"The new New England will encompass any state northeast of the New York State border, including Maine, New Hampshire, Vermont, Massachusetts, Rhode Island, and Connecticut. In its favor, the economy of New England is highly diverse and generates nearly $1 trillion per year in GDP. The members of the movement are convinced that the GDP will increase strongly once freed of the shackles of the politics and waste ridden federal government of the US.

"The new government will be based on a democratic framework with *larger local* governments and *smaller federal* governments. They plan to focus on equality, personal liberty, and environmentalism."

- "The AIP [Alaska Independence Party] is a vigorous primary pusher for secession from the United States. They argue that the original incorporation of the state was illegal, and—more importantly--that the federal government has forgotten about the Constitution of the US. They propose that Alaska—the entire state--become a completely independent nation—the sixth largest in the world based on land mass. They have done their math. The economy of Alaska will be primarily related to energy resources. Fishing, agriculture, and tourism are already vital parts of their economy and are expected to increase in financial value and in the provision of jobs.

The government of the new Republic of Alaska will be firmly a constitutional government supporting conservative, libertarian, gun ownership, and Christian ideals. Support for this movement is relatively large and strong and appears to be growing in comparison to most other movements, numbering well over 13,000 committed adherents. They will use the current state flag as their national banner."

- "The CSA [The Confederate States of America] group is by far the largest and strongest of the secessionist movements. The primary pressure group pushing the movement is the League of the South--a registered hate group. Their leader is quoted as saying, 'somebody needs to say a good word for slavery.'

"The CSA is composed of southern states including, but not limited to, South Carolina, Mississippi, Florida, Alabama, Georgia, Louisiana, and Texas. The economy has been historically agricultural--but as the movement has gained strength--it has become more industrialized. In 2013, the GDP was $5 trillion. The League of the South is on record stating that the GDP would be vastly higher if the South follows its exemplar--the former Confederacy--and allows slave labor. The movement has avowed just that intent.

"Support for the CSA is more than 25,000 dues payers, more than enough to make their petition heard."

- "Freedom Texas is the most recent and has become the most active of the US secession movements. Its goal is to separate Texas from the Union. It has significant grassroots support and numbers of volunteers. They have been working with veterans' organizations and small community groups throughout the state to begin the long process of public education about their idea of "true secession".

"Throughout the largest continental US state there has been years of lack of faith in the federal government, recent disagreement with the Affordable Care Act, and more recently and more intensely, the upholding of same-sex marriage by the Supreme Court of the US. Many formerly flag waving Texas conservatives are disenchanted and are beginning to agree with the desire to break up with the rest of the union. The directors of the movement report that almost all groups agree that an independent Texas nation is a viable goal and a real probability, no longer just a dream.

"They have a plan starting with a state referendum since Texas does not have an initiative process. The outcome of a referendum would be crucial: if it is approved, the elected Texas officials would be bound to notify Congress of people of Texas's intent to withdraw from the union. If Congress denies the initiative, a lawsuit will begin locally and finally end up in the Supreme Court.

"The second path is economic and is based on a nearly unique governmental tax law--the State of Texas has no income tax. Unlike Texas, the federal government runs a massive deficit hence there is no invasion from the

IRS. The new nation plans to implement a tariff policy. The current economy of Texas is two trillion dollars and is expected to increase by eradicating the kind of waste from which the federal government suffers. The leaders of the movement are convinced that their strong economy will be able to raise enough money to cover social security payments, military retirements, Medicare, and all direct federal programs that are contractually obligated to be paid to the people.

"The nationalist movement has over 300,000 supporters who have had the greatest successes in the cultural, economic, and political spheres throughout their state. They believe that secession is on the near horizon."

- "The Puerto Rican Independence Party remains active and continues to hold seats in the Puerto Rican Senate and House of Representatives. PR is a United States territory located just east of the Dominican Republic.

"Puerto Rico had a robust local economy largely dependent on manufacturing and real estate prior to the devastation by recent hurricanes. The state generated over $200 billion in GDP. The government of a new separate nation will be left-leaning and probably very similar to the current democratic political parties currently in power. The leaders of the movement expect to obtain at least as much GDP fiscal power as the present territory. They have two political parties, the PIP [Puerto Rican Independence Party] and the Puerto Rican Nationalist Party which do have rather different agendas. They have a partially secretive and partially open pair of movements behind independence and/or statehood—the MINH [*Movimiento Independentista Nacional*] and the FS [*Hostosiano Socialist Front*].

"Most members and believers want a peaceful transition, but there is a pair of militant organizations who advocate violence: the *Macheteros* [Boricua Popular Army] and Cadets of the Republic.

"Although there is an independence movement worthy of note, even after the hurricanes and despite their perception of ill treatment by the Trump administration, the majority of Puerto Ricans still would prefer to remain as a US territory, or better, to become a state of the United States just as Alaska and Hawaii did despite being separate from the North American continent.

"If the perception of ill treatment by the US increases, the independence movement may gain a stronger hold."

"Madam President the secessionist movements I have just described are the larger ones with the most traction, but I will conclude with a brief sentence or two about some others that are beginning to agitate within their ethnic, cultural, linguistic, and geographical regions:

- "The New Afrika movement proposes a Republic of New Afrika composed of African-Americans to occupy the entire region composed of Louisiana, Alabama, South Carolina, Georgia, and Mississippi. I really know very little about them because they are secretive and won't talk to whites.
- "In addition to the proposed new 'State of Jefferson' in California, there is another proposed state called: The Second Californian Republic or the "New"

California. It is pushed by pressure groups called Yes, California and Californians for Independence. They have two of their own political parties and California Freedom as a pressure group.

- "The Northwest Territorial Imperative movement--composed entirely of White Americans—proposes the creation of a new American state to be called the Northwest American Republic. It is sponsored by three separate—obviously related—groups, the White Aryan Resistance, Aryan Nations, and Northwestern Imperative. Like the New Afrika movement, it is race based, and secretive. You have to be a member of the club to get any information. I am informed that it doesn't hurt to have a few meaningful prison tats."

- "The Lakotah people as they prefer over the old name, Sioux, has been proposing a new state of the United States to be called the Republic of Lakotah. It will have a very small and select population.

Sybil bade the secessionists a polite goodbye, if not entirely cordial. She milled over her thoughts about what she had learned and what impact the information was having on her. She did learn a considerable amount about something she had only the haziest notion before. What she learned, she did not like. She decided that she would have a speech prepared by her speech writers to the effect that she, like Lincoln was absolutely opposed to any fractionation of the American union. She would avoid a fratricidal conflict if at all possible; but if it became necessary, she would resort to military action, as reluctantly as the 16th president had done.

As if she did not already have enough on her plate, the following morning's PDB revealed a new thorn for her to sit on. The lead item presented by DNI Admiral David P. Jacobsen was succinctly put: Kim Jong Un, the dictator of North Korea had been missing for three weeks and had not appeared in the nation's most important holiday festivities—the first absence by the Great Leaders in three generations. The DNI reported as speculation that the Shining Star of Paektu Mountain had undergone some sort of surgery. The operation had gone terribly wrong, and Chairman Kim was in a coma—maybe even an irreversible vegetative state.

As expected in the DPRK in the event of a death or incapacitation of the Father of the People, a violent succession battle was in the offing. The second most powerful person in the country, Kim's brilliant sister, Kim Yo-jong—currently serving as First Deputy Director and *de facto* leader of the Propaganda and Agitation Department of the Workers› Party of Korea, appeared to be pitted against one of several powerful generals, including: No Kwang Chol, first vice minister in the defense ministry/defense chief, Ri Yong Gil, army's chief of general staff, and Vice Marshal Ri Yong Ho, recently replaced as chief of the General Staff, but who still retains a large and loyal following--none of whom was a member of the ruling Kim family or lineage. Whoever won could likely conclude that a massive demonstration of power against the US may be necessary to demonstrate his or her bona fides.

Sybil's last thoughts before dropping off to sleep that night were, "*how did I ever get myself into such a mess?* And "*Who in her right mind would ever want to be president?*"